KATY PARKER
AND THE
HOUSE THAT CRIED

Margaret Mulligan

A & C BLACK
AN IMPRINT OF BLOOMSBURY
LONDON NEW DELHI NEW YORK SYDNEY

For Loll who always believed in K.P.

First published 2015 by
A & C Black, an imprint of Bloomsbury Publishing Plc
50 Bedford Square, London, WC1B 3DP

www.bloomsbury.com

A CIP catalogue for this book is available from the British Library

ISBN 978 1 4729 0878 0

Typeset by Newgen Knowledge Works (P) Ltd., Chennai, India
Printed and bound by CPI Group (UK) Ltd, Croydon CR0 4YY

1 3 5 7 9 10 8 6 4 2

Contents

1	The Crying Child	1
2	History Mystery	25
3	Date with Destiny	49
4	What Next?	67
5	Old School	85
6	Friend or Foe?	108
7	Settling In	121
8	The Answer	129
9	The Plan Unfolds	143
10	Reunion	154

Chapter 1

The Crying Child

Adrenalin surged through Katy's body as she ran towards the bike lying on the pavement. Reaching down, she picked it up and in one swift movement leapt onto the seat. Turning around, she called out urgently to an unseen companion, *"Hurry up! Faster! Follow me!"*

For a moment, she faltered, feet slipping off the pedals, losing precious seconds, before righting herself, then pedalling furiously ahead. The thud of her heart filled her ears.

"K-a-a-a-t-y!"

1

A terror-filled voice howled out her name as time and space seamlessly merged. Everything began to move in slow motion and all at once a mighty whoosh of blistering heat, choking smoke and blinding white light engulfed her. Katy felt herself lifted up into the air, gliding through it, weightless, limp and out of control. Within seconds she felt herself falling down, further and further into the void below.

Katy was braced for impact, fists tightly clenched, eyes squeezed shut, when with a sharp intake of breath, she jolted upright, suddenly awake.

Opening her eyes, she saw with relief the familiar surroundings of her bedroom. Sunlight seeped in beneath her curtains, casting a comforting, warm glow over the room. Katy turned to look at her bedside clock. The luminous yellow figures read six o'clock. Almost time to get up.

Sighing deeply, she sank back onto her pillow. Her body, still rigid with tension, began to relax as relief gently washed over her. It was, after all, just her dream.

Ever since her tenth birthday she had been tormented by this recurring nightmare. It followed the same pattern every year, beginning in spring and becoming more frequent, more vivid until mid-May.

Then, simply disappearing. Katy never saw who was with her or what it was she was trying to escape. Instead, she woke at precisely six o'clock every morning, just as she began to plummet into the unknown void.

Gradually, as her heart rate slowed and her breathing relaxed, Katy's mind began to wander away from her nightmare and she began to recall the previous afternoon's events with Lizzie, her best friend. They had called into the local library after school to do some research. Lizzie had found an ancient, dusty reference book, too enormous to carry, called *Dreams Unlocked*.

"Read this Katy, it fits your dream perfectly."

Katy leant over and began reading aloud, "Recurring dreams should never be ignored; they are the subconscious mind's way of trying to communicate an important message to you."

"Your message must be really important if you're having your dream so often. I wonder what it is?" said Lizzie.

Katy read on. "Dreams in which you are running away from an unseen danger are common. You must stop yourself running, turn around and face what you fear. It is your destiny. You cannot escape it."

"That's just like your dream," said Lizzie, "We've just got to figure out what you're escaping from. Are you sure you can't see who's with you? Or even recognise their voice?"

Katy squeezed her eyes tightly shut, running through the vivid images in her head. "It's hopeless," she sighed in frustration. "I've no idea. They're always just out of sight."

"Well, if what the book says is true, then a really important event or person is awaiting your arrival and, in the meantime, they're desperately trying to get your attention. You've just got to face your fear," reflected Lizzie, giving a self-satisfied smile, clearly pleased with her deductions.

Easier said than done, thought Katy, huffing crossly and pummelling her pillow.

Feeling utterly exhausted and frustrated, she pulled the covers up over her head. None of it made any sense. Last week her mum had even taken her to the doctor to see if he could help. But he had just said that she would outgrow the dream eventually and suggested a milky drink and a warm bath at bedtime, none of which seemed to make any difference. In desperation, her mum had started to sprinkle lavender water on her pillow. Apparently it was meant to promote a peaceful night's sleep. What a joke! If anything, the dream had become more frequent and even more real. Katy knew it was impossible but she was sure she could even taste smoke at the back of her throat and smell its acrid scent lingering on her nightclothes and in her hair.

Determined to make the most of the little time left before she had to get up, Katy resolutely pushed all thoughts of her dream aside. She slid her hand under her pillow and retrieved The Card. She had found it pushed under the door of her school locker and hadn't told anyone but Lizzie about it. The front of the card showed *The Kiss* by Klimt, Katy's favourite painting. She even had a poster of it on her bedroom wall. It showed a gilded couple, draped in a brilliant golden quilt. Opening it, she re-read the words written inside.

To Katy,
Meet me in room 76 tomorrow at the start of lunch. I need to talk to you.
Come on your own.
T.A xxx

Her heart began racing again but this time with excitement. Could it really be from *Tom Austin*? Would he really be waiting for her at lunch? She could see him clearly – tall and athletic, with tousled, blonde hair – he looked effortlessly cool, even in his school uniform. She imagined him inviting her to see his band playing a gig at the upcoming school talent show.

Her daydream disappeared when the all too familiar morning call from her mum interrupted her thoughts, *"Katy! Time to get up. You'll be late again if you don't get a move on!"*

Katy groaned, reluctantly rolling out of bed. Why hadn't she got up earlier? There was no time for a shower now. Wearily, she picked her uniform off the floor, where it lay in a messy heap, and quickly dressed. Still half asleep, she slammed her bedroom door behind her and raced down the stairs two at a time into the kitchen where her mum waited, wearing her usual harassed expression.

"Katy, you look as though you slept in those clothes! How many times have I told you to hang them up? Get some breakfast quickly or you'll miss the bus again."

Grabbing a piece of toast, Katy quickly waved goodbye to her mum and ran to catch the bus.

Just as Katy reached the end of the road, she turned to see her annoying little brother chasing after her down the street. Patrick ruled his year with his mad practical jokes. His unusual height made him slightly awkward and his floppy blonde fringe obscured most of his face. His current obsession centred on science fiction and he would bore you for hours, given half the chance, with his theories on time travel and parallel universes.

As Katy and Patrick got on the bus, Katy spotted Lizzie. Her hair was smooth and shiny and she even managed to look amazing in her pea-green uniform. *How does she do it?* thought Katy – and then quickly reminded herself that Lizzie probably hadn't dragged herself out of bed only moments ago. Not even Lizzie could pull off the crinkled uniform look.

* * * *

Soon the bus pulled up outside the gates of St Hilda's, a large Edwardian building in the gothic style, with hundreds of leaded windows and unusual turrets and gargoyles. Everything about the school breathed old-fashioned: from its out-dated science labs, to its hideous pea-green uniform complete with blazer. Until the 1990s boys and girls had been kept apart. They had separate entrances, classrooms and playgrounds, even eating in separate dining halls.

That morning kicked off with double science. Lesson one was a practical and in lesson two they had to write up their findings.

"Wake up, Katy, have you put the magnesium in the test tube yet?" asked Lizzie, sounding more than a little tetchy.

Katy rubbed her eyes. "Sorry, I'll do it now. I'm so tired; my stupid dream woke me up at six again this morning."

Katy picked up a bottle and haphazardly spooned some magnesium powder into the test tube while Lizzie lit the Bunsen burner and said, "Hold it over the flame until it begins to change colour. I'll be back in a minute."

Yawning, Katy did as instructed. She stared mesmerised into the flame and her surroundings seemed to melt away. A loud bang sounded, as a white light flashed in front of her eyes, followed by a strong smell of burning. Katy panicked and found herself once more in the midst of her dream. The screaming voice still called her name, getting louder and louder.

"*K-a-a-a-t-y!*"

Slowly, Katy shuddered back to the present, a cold sensation seeping over her body. Looking down, she saw her shirt was soaked through and the bottom of her tie was singed.

"W-w-hat happened?" she asked, looking around in confusion and feeling more than a little bewildered. She looked at Lizzie, who was staring back at her in astonishment. "Katy, you were on fire! Your tie was dangling in the flame – you didn't even notice!"

Katy shuddered. This was getting worse. Her dream no longer confined itself to her restless nights. It was now creeping into her waking hours. Katy, still startled, found her voice and whispered, "It was my dream. The white light took me right back into the middle of it. I could even smell burning."

Lizzie giggled, "But that's because your tie was burning, silly. You definitely need some sleep."

"Katy Parker! Stay behind when the bell goes," an icy voice cut through the crowd. Katy looked up to see Miss Harrison glaring at her.

"I can't stay behind," whispered Katy desperately to Lizzie, "I've got to meet Tom!"

"Please Miss," said Lizzie putting up her hand, "It wasn't Katy's fault, it was mine. I must have put too much magnesium in by accident."

Miss Harrison stared at Lizzie in clear disbelief before replying, "Very well, Lizzie. Write out the lab safety rules fifty times and hand them in to me in the morning."

Phew! That was close – Lizzie to the rescue again. Lizzie and Katy had met on their first day at nursery and had immediately become best friends when Lizzie heroically rescued Katy from Thomas Brown, a horrible, snotty little boy, who had been terrorising her with his dinosaur in the book corner. Lots of people commented on the unlikely pairing. Lizzie: neat and very studious. Katy, the complete opposite: always scruffy, with something ripped or in need of a wash and constantly daydreaming. But somehow they had clicked and had been inseparable ever since.

As they left the science lab, Lizzie hugged Katy. "Good luck. Meet me outside the lunch hall at one. Don't be late – I'm desperate to know what's going on!"

Katy took a deep breath to calm herself and hurried excitedly to room 76 as instructed in The Card. She still couldn't believe it. Could Tom Austin really want to meet her? Trembling all over and with butterflies swirling in her tummy, she took a deep breath, crossed her fingers for luck and entered the room.

He wasn't there. Disappointment and relief flooded over her. Checking her watch she saw she was a few minutes early so she dropped her bag on the ground and sat down on a desk in nervous anticipation, legs swinging, waiting to see what would happen next.

The room was ominously quiet. Not a sound could be heard except for the slow steady ticking of the clock on the classroom wall. Katy had just decided to give up and leave, when she heard a noise coming from the stock room. The door was slightly ajar and it definitely sounded as if something was scuffling around inside. Then, she heard an unmistakeable snort of muffled laughter. Silently sliding down from the table, Katy tiptoed over to the door and flung it open.

To her horror, she found Patrick and his group of cronies doubled over in fits of laughter, enjoying her obvious embarrassment.

"Katy loves Tom!" sang Patrick in a silly voice. "Waiting for someone important were you?" he asked, an expression of pure malice on his face.

Katy tried to hide The Card, quickly slipping it into her pocket, but too late – Patrick had seen.

"Did you really think someone like Tom Austin would be interested in you?" he jeered.

Consumed by humiliation and fury, Katy picked up her school bag and swung it at Patrick, hitting him hard in the stomach.

"I hate you!" she shouted, as Patrick winced, obviously winded, but trying to appear unhurt.

Turning to leave, she saw in dismay that a group of onlookers had gathered at the classroom door to witness her shame.

"You'll be sorry. I'll get you back! Just wait and see," she hissed through gritted teeth.

Aware of the tears welling up in her eyes, Katy began frantically pushing her way through the crowd, desperate not to be seen crying. She ran for the safety of the girls' toilets, locked herself in a cubicle and then promptly burst into tears. She remembered a time when Patrick had been her partner in crime, before he'd turned into a monster whose greatest pleasure in life seemed to be annoying her.

Moments later, the door to the toilets opened and Katy heard Lizzie's voice call, "Come out, Katy. I heard what happened."

Reluctantly, Katy slid back the bolt and opened the door. "I hate him. I knew he was planning something because I got him grounded. But how could he be so mean?"

Lizzie passed Katy a tissue and squeezed her arm. "Try and forget about it. Don't let him see he's upset you."

"OK," sniffed Katy, wiping her tear-stained face, "but you've got to help me get my own back. He'll live to regret this."

Lizzie sighed. "Alright. Let's see what we can plot in History."

* * * *

Katy enjoyed History. She loved being transported back in time and often imagined herself as a heroine in different historical settings. Her current favourite was being a spy sent behind enemy lines during the Second World War to foil some evil Nazi plot.

Katy sat with Lizzie as they listened to Mr Oakley outline their work. "Your project this half term is to investigate the Home Front during the Second World War." The usual moans and groans followed the announcement that they were getting work to do during half term. Ignoring this, Mr Oakley continued, "Try and find out what life was really like for people living in Knutsburry at the time. You can research it on the web and use the local library but it'd be really good if you could interview any locals who might have lived through the time and record their memories. There's a prize for the best project."

"Let's try and find out about Willow Dene," said Katy. "It's been abandoned since the Second World War."

"Isn't it meant to be haunted?" asked Lizzie.

"Yeah, on Halloween everyone dares each other to knock on the door. Last year the door is meant to have swung open on the third knock and they could hear a small child crying and calling out for its mummy."

"That's horrible," breathed Lizzie. "Do you think it's true?"

"My mum says it's just a rumour that's been going around for years, ever since she was little. The owners probably started it to scare kids and stop them trespassing."

"If we interview locals about the war someone is bound to know what happened at Willow Dene and if it's really haunted. Let's start interviewing on Saturday," said Lizzie.

Katy squealed with excitement, "I've got it! The perfect revenge! Let's go to Willow Dene on Saturday and take Patrick with us. We can trick him into thinking the ghost is real!"

"But how?" asked Lizzie. "He'll never believe that."

Leaning closer, Katy began to whisper her plan. "Dad is away this weekend and Mum is working on Saturday so I'm stuck with Patrick. I'll suggest we go and investigate. He won't be able to resist, especially if I make out he's too scared."

"But how will we get inside?" said Lizzie.

"I've heard that the side door is unlocked. We could give that a try."

"I'm not sure," Lizzie hesitated. "I don't want to get into trouble."

"Don't worry, it's been empty for years. No one lives there and it's not as if we're going to cause any damage," said Katy, persuasively.

"But I still don't see how we can make him think there's a ghost."

Katy stared into space concentrating hard, then smiled slyly as an idea began to take shape. "We'll download the sound of a crying child onto your phone. You slip into a room ahead of us, leaving it timed to come on a few minutes later. We'll send Patrick into the room on his own, just before the crying starts. He'll be terrified!" said Katy, a satisfied smile playing on her lips.

"Oh you are *nasty* Katy Parker! That's a great plan. Right, let's make a start on the front cover of our project," said Lizzie reaching up and getting a piece of coloured paper. "What shall we call it?"

"How about, *The House That Cried*," said Katy dramatically, already beginning to draw large jagged capital letters and colouring them in blood red.

The bell rang, signalling the end of the school day. "I've got to go and get some stuff from my locker. See you on the bus," said Katy.

"OK. I'll try and save you a seat but be quick," said Lizzie, heading for the door.

Climbing on to the bus a few minutes later, Katy looked around for Lizzie and spotted her sandwiched in on the back seat, with no room near her. Scanning the bus for a spare seat, Katy saw to her dismay that the only remaining seat was next to her horrible little brother, who was using it for his precious guitar. With a hard stare on her face, Katy walked over to him. "Move it," she demanded, pointing at the guitar. Realising Katy was in no mood to be messed with, Patrick pulled the guitar onto his lap. Desperate to avoid eye contact, they both sat in stony silence. Katy stared out of the window, waiting to see the old abandoned house.

Willow Dene was a large detached house, painted butter yellow with a deep crimson front door. It reminded Katy of a doll's house. It sat back from the road – a forbidding, high, yew hedge hid both house and garden from clear view – but from her vantage point on the bus Katy was able to peer over the hedge. The front garden looked like it might once have been an ornate rose garden. In a far corner, in the shade of a large weeping willow, stood a long abandoned swing and slide. Wrought iron gates stood imposingly at the entrance to the garden but Katy had never seen anyone going through them.

Turning to Patrick, she decided to sow the seeds of her revenge plan. "Mum is working on Saturday and

Dad will be away all weekend so I've got to look after you. Bet you're too scared to come and investigate Willow Dene. Lizzie and I are going to see if there's really a crying ghost child."

Patrick didn't answer right away. Katy could see that he was torn between a desire to see inside the mysterious old house and a fear of what they might encounter if they did.

"OK, count me in. I'm not scared. It's just an old house . . . Nothing to be worried about."

Katy hid her smile and the rest of the journey passed in silence as she thought about the coming Saturday and their planned trip to the mysterious *House That Cried*.

* * * *

Saturday morning arrived and Katy waited excitedly for Lizzie so they could discuss tactics. They had to execute the plan perfectly to give Patrick the fright of his life. At exactly ten o'clock, the doorbell rang and Katy rushed to answer it. The girls grinned at each other and then bounded up the stairs, two at a time, to Katy's bedroom.

"Is it safe to talk?" whispered Lizzie.

"Yeah, Patrick's downstairs glued to the TV and Mum has already gone to work."

Giggling, Lizzie pulled her phone out of her bag and said, "Listen to this – I downloaded it last night."

The phone emitted the eerie sound of a young child crying and desperately calling for its mummy; the chilling sound sent goosebumps up and down Katy's neck.

"That's horrible – but perfect. He'll be terrified when he hears it. We should be able to creep in the front gate, then get in by the side door. It's hidden by some overgrown bushes so no one will see us."

"I'm still not sure," said Lizzie. "You don't think it's a bit mean, do you?"

"No!" exclaimed Katy indignantly. "He deserves this. Let's scare him on the way there by telling spooky stories."

"OK, if you're sure," replied Lizzie, sounding a bit doubtful. "We'd better get going or we'll miss the bus."

Everything went according to plan to begin with. They managed to get through the gate and up the path to the side entrance of the house without being noticed.

As they reached the door, Katy suddenly felt nervous; what if they were caught? What would happen to them? Would the owner understand a harmless practical joke on an annoying little brother? She took a deep breath, pushed the door with her shoulder and turned the door handle at the same time. The door slid silently open. The silence pressed in around them as they nervously stepped inside.

It felt as if they had been transported back in time, the real world fading like a distant memory. Inside, the house looked as if time had stood still. The calendar on the wall in front of them was open to May 1942, and the 15th was circled in red.

"Weird," said Katy, "that's today's date. May 15th. I wonder why it's been circled."

Lizzie took a step backwards. "That's a bit strange, us being here on the day marked on the calendar. Do you think it's an omen? That dark forces have brought us here?" She gave a nervous giggle and reached out to grab hold of Katy's arm.

The trio slowly took in their surroundings. They were in the living room of Willow Dene. It looked like a set from one of the old films Katy liked to watch if she was off sick from school.

Facing a large open fireplace stood a faded, well-worn, brown, velvet couch with two matching armchairs. Each had a cream, lacy square of material across the back where your head would rest. Next to the fire stood a coal scuttle. The fire had been laid, ready to light. There was even a box of matches on the hearth. On the mantelpiece sat a large clock, ticking loudly, and next to it stood a pair of white china dogs. In the corner of the room stood an enormous wooden cabinet with big knobs on it.

"I know what that is," said Lizzie, walking over to the huge piece of furniture and running her hand over the smooth dark wood. "It's a radiogram. People used to listen to the radio and play records with them. Do you think it still works?"

Patrick finally spoke up in a quivering voice, "Have you noticed that everything is really clean and polished? Apart from the fact that it's in a time warp, it looks as if someone still lives here. I think we should go."

He looked at his watch, then put it to his ear. "That's weird. My watch says six o'clock; it said the right time a minute ago. What time do you make it?"

Both Katy and Lizzie looked down at their watches, then at each other in surprise, both saying in unison, "Six o'clock."

Right on cue, the clock on the mantelpiece chimed. Startled by the noise, they all looked over to the fireplace.

"What's going on?" breathed Katy, softly.

"I don't believe it," said Lizzie, sounding nervous.

They looked again at their own watches and then at the clock on the mantelpiece. All four now read exactly six o'clock.

"This place is really starting to scare me," said Katy. "Let's have a quick look round and then get out of here."

Shivering, Lizzie nodded in agreement whilst hugging herself and rubbing her arms vigorously.

"What's happened now?" she said. "It's freezing. It was nice and warm a minute ago."

Before anyone had a chance to reply, they all stopped dead in their tracks as they heard a door slam loudly. The three of them looked at one another, open-mouthed in fright.

"What was –" Katy started to say, when an eerie noise silenced her: quiet at first and hard to make out but gradually getting louder and louder. It seemed to be coming from upstairs. Katy could hear the sound of a weeping child, quickly followed by desperate cries for mummy. For what seemed like an eternity, all three stood frozen to the spot, hearts pounding, barely able to breathe. Then, suddenly, as if released from a spell, they turned and ran outside, slamming the door shut behind them.

They didn't stop running until they reached the end of the street and the shelter of the bus stop. Patrick had moved beyond terrified. His face had turned a sickly shade of white and he could hardly speak as he visibly shook from head to foot.

"What just happened?" gasped Lizzie, trying to catch her breath.

Katy shook her head, her eyes wide with fear. "I have no idea. But I'd better get Patrick home. He doesn't look too well."

Katy hailed an oncoming bus and with one last worried look at her friend she jumped on board, dragging an ashen-faced Patrick behind her.

Once they arrived home, Patrick refused to discuss the incident, putting on a brave face and retreating to the front room to watch TV.

Katy left Patrick and snuck off to ring Lizzie. "Brilliant. You even had me fooled for a minute or two! I wasn't expecting you to play the crying child when you did. Awesome acting too, by the way. You looked totally terrified! The door slamming when it did was great timing."

A deathly silence followed at the other end of the phone. Then, finally, Lizzie spoke in a strange, small voice. "Stop it Katy, you're scaring me. You know I didn't make the crying sound. My phone went dead. I couldn't get it to work. Stop messing about. I thought it was you!"

For a moment, Katy felt sick with fear. Had it really been the ghost? Or was someone playing a trick on them? She took a deep breath and decided there and then that they had to go back to Willow Dene and find out for sure.

Chapter 2

History Mystery

The following week flew by, as May half term approached. Both Katy and Lizzie reluctantly decided to put all thoughts of Willow Dene aside for the next few days. Their exams were coming up and Katy felt the pressure mounting. They agreed to go back and investigate as soon as possible. Katy still felt a little scared. At night, lying in bed, she relived the experience over and over. The tiny hairs on her arms stood on end and her heart beat faster as she remembered the door slamming and the haunting cries of the child. In the morning, she woke up tired and found it harder than ever to concentrate in class, her every waking minute consumed by thoughts of her dream and the crying child.

Finally, the moment Katy had been longing for arrived. The last lesson of the last day of school: History, with Mr Oakley. They spent the lesson preparing questions for their project on the Home Front, which was due in after the holiday.

"When shall we start our interviews?" asked Katy.

"Mum thinks Sunday afternoon, just after lunch, would be best. She reckons people will be relaxing in their gardens with time to talk," answered Lizzie.

"OK. We'll start with some general questions about rationing and evacuees, then move onto questions about Willow Dene."

The bell rang and the class cheered – finally the holidays had arrived.

"At last," sighed Lizzie, "I thought we'd never break up."

"I know," grinned Katy, "a full week off. Mum said the heatwave is meant to last all next week, too."

"Brilliant! Once we've started on our project, let's go to the lido and sunbathe and swim all day."

"Definitely," Katy agreed. "I need a break – every morning I wake up feeling exhausted. My dream is getting worse, not better."

As the girls walked to the bus stop, they finalised the plans for their project.

"Remember, we're meeting on Sunday at the bus stop at two o'clock. Don't forget your dad's video camera for filming the interviews. Are you sure we can borrow it?"

"I'm sure it'll be fine but Patrick better be careful with it. Is he still doing the filming for us?"

"Yeah, my mum will be at work and Dad has to go away again so I've got to bring him with me," replied Katy.

Katy wasn't sure she had forgiven Patrick just yet but realised he would be useful to have around. He seemed to have a way with older people. They liked him and that would be useful if they were going to get some good interviews.

"I hope we find out some more about Willow Dene. I can't stop thinking about what happened there," said Katy.

"Someone's bound to know," answered Lizzie, breezily, "and before you start, there's no such thing as ghosts. So stop worrying about it, silly!"

"I suppose you're right," mumbled Katy, secretly not so sure.

* * * *

Sunday morning dawned bright and sunny. Katy had suffered another fitful night's sleep. Her dream had now become so vivid, that when she awoke it was hard to distinguish it from reality. Sitting up in bed, Katy felt a stab of pain in her leg and reached down to rub it. She felt both puzzled and alarmed to see nasty, red grazes all down her left shin and arm. Katy had absolutely no recollection as to where or when she had hurt herself. Neither injury was there when she went to sleep the previous night. Starting to panic, she noticed that the deep graze in her leg even appeared to have bits of gravel in it and her sheet was marked with flecks of dried blood where she must have rubbed against it in her sleep. What was going on? Could it be possible that her dream was somehow real? It certainly felt that way. Leaning over and trying to not to touch her sore arm on the bed, she picked up her glass of water from the bedside table. Katy took a long drink, desperate to sooth her parched and scratchy throat and rid it of the lingering taste of smoke. Cuts on her arm and leg and tasting smoke in the morning – there was something seriously wrong here. Feeling dazed and confused, Katy climbed gingerly out of bed and made her way to the bathroom, limping slightly.

"What's the matter, Katy?" asked her mum, appearing out of nowhere at the top of the stairs.

Katy had no idea what was going on – how was she going to explain where the cuts had come from? Not wanting to worry her mum before she knew what was happening, she muttered, "It's nothing," and tried to move past her.

"Come here, let me look," insisted her mum, grabbing Katy by the sore arm and making her cry out loud in pain. "How on earth did you do this?" she asked in concern.

Katy blurted out the first thing that came into her mind. "I fell off my bike." As she spoke, she realised she was describing her dream but not reality.

"You need to be more careful," her mum cautioned. "There's some antiseptic cream in the bathroom cabinet, make sure you give it a good clean."

"Yes, Mum," Katy moaned in reply.

"Don't forget I've got work today so you need to take Patrick with you when you go out."

"Yeah, I know, he's going to do the filming for us," replied Katy.

"Good. Make sure you're back for tea at five and don't get into any trouble."

* * * *

Katy and Patrick got the bus to meet Lizzie. Patrick rang the bell, they stumbled down the stairs from the top deck and hopped off to find Lizzie waiting patiently for them. She gave Katy a big smile and Patrick a friendly thump.

"Come on, you two, thought you'd never get here. Got the questions, Katy?"

Feeling pleased with herself, Katy pulled out a folder with the questions typed up. "How professional am I?" she said, giving Lizzie her questions with a flourish.

"Have you got the video camera?" asked Patrick, eager to get his hands on it.

"Yeah, here it is," said Lizzie, taking it out of her bag. "Be careful with it or my dad will kill me."

"Come on then, let's get started," said Katy, striding off purposefully ahead of the others, already halfway up someone's drive.

They spent the next hour knocking on doors and getting the low-down on life during the war. Some of it was quite interesting, especially the stuff about nettle soup and dried eggs. It sounded horrible but, funnily enough, people seemed to remember those days fondly. Most had moved to Knutsburry long after the war and so had no knowledge of Willow Dene except to say it had always been empty and what a shame that was as it was such a pretty family house.

"Right that's it, I give up," moaned Katy grumpily, sitting down on the pavement and flinging her notepad aside. "No one seems to know anything about Willow Dene. It's hopeless!"

"Why don't we try number 32?" asked Patrick, attempting to sound brave.

Katy and Lizzie both stared at him, momentarily speechless.

"Are you mad?" asked Lizzie, shaking her head in disbelief.

"You do know who lives there, don't you?" asked Katy.

"Yeah," answered Patrick, "just some weird old lady. It's not like she's a real witch," he smirked. "Unless, of course, you two actually believe in witches?"

Katy and Lizzie looked at each other uncertainly. Local children feared the old woman who lived at number 32. They hurried past her house, too scared to walk slowly in case she magically appeared and cast some unspeakable spell on them. Sinister myths had sprung up surrounding this shadowy, rarely seen figure and were now woven into the fabric of local folklore.

"What do you think?" asked Lizzie, twisting her hair around her finger nervously. "Isn't she meant to be connected to Willow Dene in some way?"

"I've never seen her," said Katy. "They say when Willow Dene was abandoned she went mad and disappeared into her house, only coming out under the cover of night."

Patrick rolled his eyes in ridicule and laughed. "You two are such big babies! If you really want to find out about Willow Dene, I reckon she's just the person you need to speak to. Are you coming or not?"

Reluctantly, Katy and Lizzie followed him up the drive to number 32. Patrick picked up the heavy brass knocker and banged firmly on the door twice, then quickly retreated behind the girls. Not a sound could be heard.

"No one's in," sighed Katy in relief. "Look, all the curtains are shut. Let's go."

"Wait a minute, look there," instructed Lizzie, pointing to an upstairs bedroom window.

Katy looked up, just in time to see a pair of dark eyes peering out from behind the curtain. Summoning up all her courage, she knocked one more time. All three waited with bated breath to see what would happen next. Footsteps could be heard approaching the door, followed by the sound of the latch being lifted, then finally the door began to creak open and a small, dark, bent figure came into view.

Lizzie gave a shrill scream, jumping backwards into a startled Katy, who then, spooked by Lizzie, also screamed, clutching onto her in terror.

"How can I help you, children?" asked a gentle voice.

Katy turned back to the dark figure. There, on the doorstep, stood a tiny, old lady, stooped and twisted with age. She wore an old fashioned, sombre black dress, as if she were in mourning for those long dead. It was easy to see why she had a reputation for being a witch.

Undaunted, Patrick spoke up. "Hello. We're doing a project on life during the Second World War for school and we're interviewing locals about their experiences."

"We wondered if you could help us?" asked Lizzie, smiling nervously and looking embarrassed by her scream.

"Did you live here during the War?" asked Katy, taking out her questionnaire.

The years seemed to melt away on the old woman's face, as she broke into an unexpectedly warm smile. "I'm Hillary and yes I've lived here all my life. I can remember the War being declared. Lovely sunny afternoon it was too. Just like today."

She proceeded to tell them all sorts of interesting stories about rationing and the blackout.

"Can you tell us anything about Willow Dene," asked Katy, innocently. "Do you know why it was abandoned? Or anything about the rumours of the crying child?"

Storm clouds seemed to gather overhead and the air turned cold as Hillary's smile vanished, replaced by a look of such profound sadness that Katy had to look away. Hillary visibly shrank backwards, whispered a hoarse goodbye and swiftly shut the door.

They stared at one another in surprise, until Katy spoke. "What just happened?"

"That was strange. She chatted happily until you asked about Willow Dene. Something terrible must have happened there and she must be tied up with it to react like that," suggested Patrick.

"But what?" mused Lizzie.

"Well, I'm going to find out. Come on, let's carry on with our research. Why don't we go back to number 83? It's the only house left we haven't been to. They were out earlier but someone might be in now who can fill us in with the full story," said Katy, filled with determination.

Number 83 was called Cedar Cottage, presumably due to the huge cedar tree in the front garden. It was a pretty, white cottage, with blue shutters, a yellow front door and a red climbing rose growing up the side of the house.

"Come on," said Katy, opening the garden gate and walking up the path to the front door. She gave the bell a long hard ring. They waited and waited for someone to answer.

"There's still no one in," huffed Katy, grumpily. "Come on let's go."

Just as they were heading off back down the path, the door suddenly opened and there, to

Katy's amazement, stood Tom Austin. Katy gulped, struggling to speak, as Tom stood there, staring expectantly at them.

"I assume you rang the bell because you wanted to speak to someone?" he asked.

Silence followed.

Lizzie came to Katy's rescue. "We're interviewing locals for our history project; we really want to find out about Willow Dene. It's been empty since the War but no one seems to know why."

"Well, you've come to the right house. My granddad is in the garden and he's lived in Knutsburry all his life. He looks after Willow Dene for the owners, so if he can't tell you what happened there, no one can. Follow me."

He led them down a winding path that ran along the side of the house and into the large back garden. They passed by flowerbeds bursting full of colourful flowers and rows of fruit trees. Tom's granddad, Charlie, was sitting on an old stripy deckchair, drinking a mug of tea at the back of the garden. He looked up, giving them a welcoming smile.

"Hello there, what an honour! No one under eighty calls for me these days!"

Patrick took a step forward and spoke up. "Hello sir. My sister and her friend are interviewing local people for a history project about life during the Second World War. We'd really like to find out about Willow Dene but no one seems to know anything and we wondered if you could help."

It was just about the longest speech Katy had ever heard Patrick give and she stared at him in amazement. Maybe he wasn't so useless after all!

The old man gestured for them to sit down on the grass, then took a long drink of his tea before beginning. "Call me Charlie. No need to stand on ceremony with me. Well, where shall I begin? Lived here all my life. Born here you see and just sort of stayed put. My wife liked it; said it was a good family home. Course my children have long gone, all grown up now with kids of their own, like Tom here. He's my grandson."

"So you remember when Willow Dene was still lived in, then?" Katy interrupted.

Charlie chuckled. "Of course. It doesn't seem that long ago to an old man like me."

"Can you tell us about the people who lived there?" Lizzie said.

Charlie smiled wistfully as he replied. "My best mates, the twins, Harry and Frank lived there. They were great fun – always dragging me into some mischief or other. Their dad was the local doctor and his wife, Mrs Graham, took in evacuees when the War started."

Charlie paused and smiled to himself as he remembered happy times. "They had a lovely little sister called Susie, a real favourite with everyone. Always singing and playing out in the street with her skipping rope or pushing a pram filled with dolls up and down the pavement."

"Why was the house abandoned?" asked Katy. "Is it really haunted by a crying child?"

Charlie sighed deeply, clasping his mug tightly, and then began his tale. "Bit of a quiet war here, really. Not much happened in the way of action to get us boys excited. We'd rush out to watch the German Junkers on their way to bomb Liverpool. Hundreds of them, it seemed to us boys. Later you could see the whole city ablaze, the sky would glow with fires from incendiary bombs. Exciting for us: far enough away to be safe but close enough to view the action."

"Wow that must have been amazing. Nothing exciting like that ever happens now," blurted out Patrick.

"Only one bomb ever dropped here and, after seeing the death and destruction it caused, it was one too many by my reckoning. Didn't go out and watch Liverpool burning night after night with such excitement after that."

"What happened?" asked Patrick.

Charlie paused as he remembered the night in question. Then, leaning towards them, he began his tale in a hushed, grave voice. "I'll never forget the date: May 15th, 1942. It was a lovely warm evening, with clear skies and a warm breeze. You could hear it blowing gently through the trees. It started off like any other normal evening; I'd just got home from my paper round at about six o'clock, when I heard an enemy aircraft flying in low. Us boys could identify the different planes by the sound they made."

Patrick inched closer to Charlie and gazed at him in open admiration. Charlie absent-mindedly leant down and patted him on the shoulder, then continued with his story. "It was closer than usual and seemed to be heading for the High Street. Within minutes, the sirens started to sound and we went to shelter in the cellar."

"What was it like? Were you scared? Did you think you were going to die?" Patrick asked, excitedly.

"We certainly spent a very tense hour down there, not knowing what was happening above ground or what to expect when the all-clear was sounded. But we played cards, Mum sang songs and my dad played his harmonica."

"I don't know how you could stand it. I'd be terrified! Was everyone alright?" asked Lizzie.

Charlie cleared his throat and continued his story. "When the all clear sounded, I rushed upstairs and straight out onto the street to see what had happened. Victoria Avenue was fine but there was a lot of shouting and screaming coming from the High Street."

"What did you do?" asked Lizzie

"I raced off to investigate, before my mum could stop me." Charlie paused briefly, his face now etched with anguish as he remembered the events of that evening. "The main thing I remember is the smoke and the awful smell of burning – that and the sound of people wailing and crying. Then, I heard the voices of the twins, Harry and Frank, above everyone else's. They were calling for their little sister, over and over until they were hoarse with shouting."

"What had happened to her?" asked Katy, anxiously.

"Mrs Graham had taken the new evacuees to the cinema for a treat, leaving the twins at home in bed recovering from chickenpox. My cousin Hillary from number 32 had come round to keep an eye on them and babysit Susie, who was only three years old, about to be four."

Charlie's voice sounded choked as he struggled to continue his tale. "Beautiful little thing she was, all curly blonde hair and big blue eyes, but quite mischievous at times." A sad smile flickered across his face.

The group fell silent until Lizzie found her voice. "Was she OK?"

"When the siren sounded, the twins were upstairs asleep. Realising what was happening, they rushed downstairs to join Susie and Hillary in the cellar, which was kitted out as an air raid shelter. They were surprised that Hillary hadn't come to get them when the siren went off but when they ran into the kitchen they discovered why. They found her unconscious on the kitchen floor."

Lizzie gasped. "What happened to her? Was it a burglar?"

"No. Turned out she had panicked when she heard the siren. She stumbled, fell and hit her head hard on the grate. The twins found the front door wide open and little Susie nowhere to be found. They were about to chase after her when an air raid warden spotted them and marched them off to the cellar. By the time they were able to search, pandemonium had broken out – ambulances and sirens wailing everywhere."

Charlie stopped speaking, put down his tea, stood up and made his way over to his potting shed. Patrick, eager to find out more from Charlie, leapt up and followed him inside, leaving the girls sitting on the grass.

Tom took up the story where Charlie had left off. "Granddad doesn't like to remember this part but I know what happened. The cinema took a direct hit that night. Everyone was killed, not one single survivor. Lots of Granddad's school friends died that night, as well as Mrs Graham and her evacuees. As for Susie . . . no one ever found out what happened to her. She was put down as missing, presumed dead.

They reckon that when the siren sounded and Hillary fell and hit her head, Susie got a fright and wandered out into the street, making her way up to the cinema trying to find Mrs Graham. She must have got caught up in the blast."

The girls fell silent for a moment. Katy couldn't get over how sad it all was. After a while she said, "But that doesn't explain why the house has always been empty."

"Soon afterwards, Dr Graham came home from the War, collected the twins and left. They never returned and left everything behind. Granddad thinks that Dr Graham couldn't bear to be in the house; it was too painful, a reminder of the happy family they'd once been."

"Why didn't he just sell it?" asked Lizzie.

"Granddad thinks Dr Graham wanted it to be there waiting for Susie, just as it was when she left that evening. That's why the house looks like it's frozen in time now. They left everything behind, so it would look exactly the same for Susie."

"We just met Hillary," said Lizzie. "Is that why she never comes out and wears black? Everyone thinks she's a witch."

Tom gave them a sad look. "Yeah, she blamed herself for Susie's disappearance – never got over it. Just retreated into herself and soon the stories began. Even I used to be a bit scared of her."

Charlie reappeared from his potting shed with a faded postcard in his hand and Patrick at his side. "This is from Frank and Harry, the twins. We still keep in touch. They moved to Filey in Yorkshire after it happened and they still live there now. This card has their address on it. Why don't you write to them and ask if you can have a look around Willow Dene? It's just as it was during the War. My mum used to go in and dust around the place once a month to keep things in good condition. When it got too much for her I took over; I still take care of it now."

"I'd love that," said Katy, "Do you think they'll let us look around?"

"Yes, if I'm with you. You could get some good photos for your project: show how ordinary people lived during the War. Mind you, the Grahams were better off than most. There are even clothes still hanging up in the wardrobe. You could dress up and take photos of yourselves for a bit of fun."

"Yeah, that's a good idea," said Lizzie. Katy could tell that Lizzie was thinking of the mark they might get at school if they handed in a truly unique project.

"We'll write to them this evening. Thanks, Charlie, you've been brilliant."

Patrick looked at his watch and cried out in surprise, "Oh no, it's almost five o'clock. Mum will be mad if we're late for tea."

"I'll show you out through the front," said Charlie. "I've a photo you might like to see. Follow me."

Charlie led them through the kitchen and into the hallway. On a small, wooden table stood countless picture frames. Charlie picked up an old, black and white photograph in a silver frame and handed it to Katy. "Thought you might like to see this; it's the Graham family outside Willow Dene."

The photograph showed Willow Dene with a happy smiling family standing outside the gates. The dad stood laughing, leaning on his bike, while his wife stood with her arms around two young boys, aged about eleven or twelve. In front of them sat a very pretty little girl of about three, with curly hair in two bunches.

It was really strange. Katy had the strongest feeling that she knew them. They all looked so very familiar. But that was impossible – this picture had been taken long ago, before she was even born. "Do you know when it was taken?" she asked.

Charlie closed his eyes in concentration. "Yes, I think it was taken in April 1942, when Dr Graham came home on leave for a few days, just before everything started to go wrong for them. A happy day it was too."

Charlie went quiet and Katy was sure she saw a tear glistening on his cheek. Then, in the blink of an eye, his whole mood changed again and he was back to his usual, jovial self. "Let me know if you hear from the twins."

Katy, Lizzie and Patrick waved goodbye to Charlie and made their way back down the garden path.

* * * *

Lizzie went back to Katy's for tea that afternoon. Afterwards, they went upstairs to Katy's bedroom to write their letter. After several attempts, they were finally happy with their work.

Dear Frank and Harry,

Our names are Lizzie Mullins and Katy Parker and we are currently attending St Hilda's in your hometown of Knutsburrry, Cheshire. We have been researching what life was like on the Home Front during the Second World War and would be very interested to have a look around your old home, Willow Dene. Your friend, Charlie Robinson, suggested we write to you and ask your permission to take some photographs of the house and use them to illustrate our project. Please could you write back and let us know if this is possible?

Yours sincerely,
Katy Parker and Lizzie Mullins

They put the letter in an envelope, then borrowed a stamp from Katy's mum and set off to the post box on the corner.

"I really hope they get in touch and say yes. I'd love to go back to Willow Dene and have a proper look inside," said Lizzie.

"I know, me too," replied Katy. "But I hope nothing spooky happens this time. Now we know what happened to Susie, I keep thinking it's her we heard crying. Crying for her mum, still lost."

Lizzie gave her a gentle push and laughed nervously. "You've been reading too many horror stories. There's no such thing as ghosts and you know it!"

Katy smiled uncertainly. Something or someone was waiting for her at Willow Dene. She felt certain of that but who or what remained a mystery. All Katy knew was that she felt powerless to resist.

Chapter 3

Date with Destiny

As the end of the holiday approached, Katy had almost given up on hearing from the twins when Lizzie texted her early Friday evening.

Heard from Harry & Frank, call me!

Katy rang her immediately, "What did it say? Will they let us go to Willow Dene?"

Lizzie read her the reply.

Dear Lizzie and Katy,

We were very pleased to receive your letter and are interested to hear that you are doing a project on the Home Front during the Second World War. Sometimes it seems that we are the only ones who still remember that time. We have written to Charlie to tell him that it's fine for him to show you around our old home, Willow Dene. We hope you find it of some use. Perhaps you could send us a copy of your project and any photos you take of our old home. It was a happy place to live before the war and that is how we like to remember it.

Good luck with your project.

Best Wishes,
Frank and Harry Graham.

"Brilliant! Let's go on Sunday morning and then we can write up our project in the afternoon. I've promised Patrick he can come with us if he does the dishes all next week."

* * * *

On Sunday morning, Katy's heart sank as she looked in the mirror to wash her face. A large, red graze had appeared out of nowhere on her left cheek. "Not again," she muttered, panic coursing through her once more. She still hadn't come up with a good way to explain the appearance of all these cuts to her mum. Luckily, she almost managed to disguise it with some of her mum's make-up and partly hide it beneath her thick hair. That would keep her mum from asking any more questions.

Katy and Patrick set off excitedly, meeting Lizzie along the way. They were all eager to explore Willow Dene further but they were also a little nervous of what they might encounter after the last time. Standing at the gate, with a warm smile on his face, stood Charlie. "Come on then, follow me. Let's take a trip down memory lane!"

This time, they entered the house through the large, red, wooden front door, which had a stained glass fanlight over the top. They found themselves standing in a large central hall with a huge winding wooden staircase in front of them. The floor was covered with black and white tiles and along one wall stood a bamboo wooden table. Upon this was a large golden lamp with tassels and the same black and white photograph of the Graham family that Charlie had at his house. Next to the table, stood an old-fashioned coat stand, which eerily still held a couple of coats, including a small child's duffle coat. It felt as if the owners were still at home.

"I'll give you a guided tour and point out anything that might help with your project. We'll start with the cellar first. This way. Be careful on the steps. The Grahams used the cellar as an air raid shelter. You should get some good pictures for your project down here."

The children followed Charlie down a flight of steep steps and into the musty smelling cellar deep below.

"This is amazing," gasped Katy, as she looked about her in surprise. The cellar was still equipped with bunk beds, candles and tins of food. There were even playing cards set out on a small wooden table, as if at any moment the players might return to finish the game. A newspaper lay open on one of the bunks.

Katy picked it up to look at the date, "Look at this," she whispered to Lizzie, holding up the newspaper for her to see. "It's the same date again. May 15th! It's as if the house is stuck in time, reliving the same terrible day over and over." With this thought she shivered.

"Come on, I'll show you the rest of the house. Don't be so gloomy. I like to remember it as a happy house. I hope it can be again one day."

After a look at the kitchen and parlour, as Charlie called it, he led them upstairs and onto the spacious landing. "Willow Dene is not your typical house," explained Charlie. "The family were quite well off. Most people didn't have indoor toilets but the Grahams had two bathrooms. It amazed me as a kid."

"Can you guess who this room belonged to?" asked Charlie.

"The twins," said Patrick immediately, as he looked about in admiration at an army of soldiers set out on the floor ready to do battle. From the ceiling hung model aeroplanes. Charlie proudly reeled off their names, "Spitfire, Lancaster, Hurricane." In the corner lay a couple of tennis rackets, a cricket bat and some stumps.

"Come on," said Katy, dragging Patrick out of the room. "Keep up!"

"This was Susie's room," said Charlie, pushing the door open and stepping inside, a sad smile on his face.

"It looks as if she's just left," gasped Katy.

The room had pale yellow wallpaper with small blue butterflies, and curtains to match. In the centre of the room stood a small, metal-framed, white bed, complete with a pink patchwork quilt, upon which lay a baby doll with a dummy in its mouth. On the floor, a doll's tea set had been laid out, waiting for the long overdue guests to arrive.

Charlie led them back out onto that landing and opened the next door. "And here's Mr and Mrs Graham's bedroom," he said.

"It's beautiful," Katy said, walking into the room for a closer look. The walls were papered with delicate blue forget-me-nots on a cream background. The bed, a huge wooden four-poster, was dressed with faded curtains that matched the wallpaper. In the large bay window stood an elegant white dressing table, upon which were several ornate glass perfume bottles and a matching silver hairbrush and hand-mirror.

As if in a trance, Katy walked across the room and sat down at the dressing table. She removed the stopper from a perfume bottle and raised it to her nose. She could just make out the aroma of faded violets and lavender. Closing her eyes, she inhaled deeply. Quite suddenly, the fleeting but powerful image of a smiling lady with fair hair and blue eyes filled her mind's eye, then swiftly disappeared. Feeling a little woozy, Katy stood up shakily. "What was Mrs Graham like?" she asked, resting one hand on the dressing table as the room span around her.

Charlie paused, staring into the distance. "She was a lovely lady. A real second mother to me and all the evacuees she took in. I've got a feeling she would have liked you. There's a portrait of her hanging on the landing. Come on, I'll show you."

Katy paused to take a final look around the room. Hanging on the back of the door she noticed two dressing gowns: a woollen, navy-blue one, which she guessed had been Dr Graham's and a red silk kimono decorated with yellow humming birds. There were even slippers, still half-tucked under the bed.

Katy thought that the house felt warm and welcoming on this visit, as if it was glad to finally receive invited guests after so many years of silence.

"Come on, Katy," urged Lizzie. "Charlie's waiting on the landing."

Shaking her head, Katy followed Lizzie out of the room. She felt confused and thick headed; what was wrong with her now?

Charlie stood in front of a small faded oil painting. "This is Mrs Graham. The painting was done in Paris on their honeymoon."

Katy's heart lurched as she stared, mesmerized by the familiar pretty face smiling at her out of the portrait. It couldn't be could it? The same blue eyes and blonde hair that she had just conjured up on smelling the perfume. Charlie interrupted her thoughts. "Come back downstairs. I've got a surprise for you."

They followed Charlie into the dining room, where the table had been laid for tea. "I thought you'd enjoy a wartime tea, to help you get the feel of life during the War. You can dress up in some of the children's old clothes if you like. Mrs Graham always kept some ready for evacuees. Sometimes they would turn up with nothing but what they stood up in. The clothes are in the wardrobe in the back bedroom."

"Thanks, Charlie," said Lizzie, nudging Katy, who seemed to be in a daze. "I'm starving."

"I've got some of my favourite wartime tunes here for you to listen to," he said, pointing to a pile of old records. "I'll just show you how to use the radiogram and then leave you to it. I'll be back at five o'clock to tidy and lock up."

After a quick demonstration, Charlie called out, "Have fun," and then left, shutting the door behind him.

"Come on, sleepy head, let's get dressed up like Charlie said," giggled Lizzie, racing upstairs to the back bedroom. Katy followed behind slowly, mulling things over before deciding not to say anything in front of Patrick. It sounded too weird to explain and she didn't quite trust him yet.

In the bedroom, Lizzie flung open the wardrobe door and began to rummage through the clothes hanging on the rail.

"What's that smell?" asked Katy, sniffing the sleeve of what looked like a pea green St Hilda's school cardigan.

"It's just moth balls," replied Lizzie knowledgeably, "I recognise the smell from my gran's house. She uses them in her wardrobe to stop moths eating her jumpers. Here, put on these shorts, this shirt and tank top," said Lizzie, handing a pile of clothes to

Patrick. "You'll need these long grey socks and look, there's even a cap you can wear!"

"OK," answered Patrick reluctantly, "but you'd better get dressed up too. I'm not going to be the only one looking stupid."

"Don't worry. I've found a couple of checked dresses here, with cardigans and some long white socks for us to wear."

Katy groaned. "Do we have to?"

"Yes," replied Lizzie with authority. "I want us to win the prize for this project and we stand more chance if we're original."

Reluctantly, Katy got changed and even agreed to let Lizzie put her hair into two bunches, tied with matching blue bows.

"Don't forget this," instructed Lizzie, throwing a hand-knitted woollen cardigan across the room to Katy, where it landed at her feet. Katy bent over to pick it up and noticed something half dangling out of the pocket.

"Look at this – it was in the pocket," she said, showing Lizzie a delicate silver watch on a well-worn, soft, black leather strap. "I wonder how long it's been in this pocket and who it belonged to?"

Lizzie reached out and took it from her for a closer look. Katy watched Lizzie's expression change from one of mild interest to wide-eyed surprise as she handed the watch back. "Check out the date and time the watch stopped."

Katy looked at the watch face and saw, the date 15th May, 1942. The tiny hands had stopped dead on six o'clock, too. Lizzie and Katy stared at each other in surprise, too stunned to speak.

"Stop being stupid you two! Old watches like this need winding every day or they stop. We know the family moved out after the bombing, that's why the watch has stopped on that date. No one's worn it since. Give it here," instructed Patrick, authoritatively.

Katy handed it over to Patrick, who quickly wound it up and adjusted it until it said the correct date and time. "Here you go, put it on," he instructed, passing it back.

"Yeah, it goes with the old-fashioned outfit. It makes it more authentic somehow," added Lizzie.

Katy reluctantly fastened the watch on her wrist and momentarily stopped in her tracks as the dream flashed in front of her eyes again. For a split second, she almost caught a glimpse of her companion, cycling behind her. Just as their face began to come into view, she felt a hand shaking her shoulder and the image vanished.

"Katy, what's the matter with you today? You keep zoning out," huffed Lizzie, losing patience.

"Nothing. I'm just tired, that's all," insisted Katy, determined to put on brave face in front of Patrick.

Turning to look in the mirror, she laughed. "Argh, we look ridiculous!"

"I bet my mum would think we look lovely," said Lizzie. "She's always moaning that I dress too old for my age."

Lizzie stood staring at Patrick and Katy. "It's strange, you two seem to suit these clothes. I reckon you'd fit right in. I just look weird."

"Cheeky!" laughed Katy. "Are you saying we're naturally old-fashioned?"

"I know," said Patrick. "I'll film you, then you can show your mum what you look like as someone from the 1940s!" Patrick took out the camera and started filming.

After ten minutes, Katy had had enough. "Come on, I'm starving. Let's go and eat," she said, leaving the bedroom and heading back downstairs into the dining room.

"Listen to this," said Lizzie, putting on a record and dragging Katy up to dance. Patrick jumped up to join in and all three of them began trying to outdo one another with silly dances, until, finally, they collapsed on the rug, too exhausted to continue.

"Come on, let's eat," said Katy.

Patrick picked up a note from the table and read it aloud.

This is the sort of tea we could only have on special occasions during the war, as so many foods were rationed. The Grahams, however, usually ate better than most as they had their own hens and a goat, as well as a small vegetable plot of their own. You were usually sure of a good tea at their table. It was a standing joke that I always knocked on the door as the table was being laid for supper.

Enjoy!
Charlie

On the table lay a loaf of freshly baked crusty bread that smelt delicious, along with plenty of butter and a jar of Charlie's homemade strawberry jam. There were also hard-boiled eggs, slices of ham, big chunks of cheddar cheese and an enormous jug of homemade lemonade, which they all gulped down thirstily.

They were chatting happily when Lizzie, glancing at the clock on the mantelpiece, called out in alarm. "Oh no, I'm going to be late! I promised Mum I'd be home by half four to walk the dog. It's my birthday next week so I've got to stay in her good books until then."

Lizzie raced upstairs and quickly changed back into her own clothes, before calling out "goodbye."

"What do you want to do now?" asked Patrick. "We don't need to be home for another hour yet."

"Let's stay until five o'clock when Charlie will be back. I want to look through these old magazines and photo albums. I might find some pictures to use in my project," replied Katy, picking up a large, red, leather album.

"It's too quiet," said Patrick walking over to the radiogram. "I'll see if I can tune this old thing into the twenty-first century."

After ten minutes of messing about with the dials, they successfully found their favourite music station.

Katy lay on the carpet, happily flicking through old fashion magazines, while Patrick sat on the couch with a pile of old comics.

* * * *

They both must have fallen asleep, as it was some time later that Katy suddenly jolted awake, momentarily unsure of where she was. Patrick lay, snoring gently, on the couch. Katy leant over and shook him roughly by the shoulder. "Wake up Patrick, we must have fallen asleep. Why hasn't Charlie come back for us?"

Patrick slowly opened his eyes, glaring at her as he rubbed his shoulder. "You don't have to be so rough." He stretched and sat up, looking equally confused at his surroundings. "That was weird, us falling asleep like that," he said. "It must have been all that food. Come on, let's get changed. Mum will worry if we're late."

They sat side by side for a few moments, trying to summon the energy to get moving. Suddenly, Patrick noticed something strange. "Listen! What's happened to the radio?"

"Why, what's the matter?"

"Just listen," said Patrick.

The voice speaking on the radio sounded odd. It was clipped and precise, old-fashioned even, like someone from one of the old black and white films Katy liked to watch. They listened as Big Ben chimed and the radio presenter announced the six o'clock news. Katy and Patrick stared at each other in disbelief as they listened to the headlines.

"This is the six o'clock news read by Ralph Robinson, reporting live from the BBC, on Sunday 12th April, 1942." The voice went on to report bombings in London and Liverpool.

Katy glanced nervously down at the watch on her wrist. Her eyes widened in shock. This couldn't be happening . . . the watch must be wrong. She quickly tried to hide both her panic and the watch from Patrick but she wasn't fast enough.

"Show me," he demanded.

Reluctantly, Katy turned the watch face towards him. Patrick's mouth fell wide open and he looked at Katy. His face had gone pale and his voice began to shake as he spoke. "That's impossible. I just set it to today's date. Why does it say 12th April, 1942? That's the same date the radio announcer just said, isn't it? What's happening Katy?"

"I don't know. It must be some sort of joke programme, you know, like an April Fool," Katy replied, squeezing his hand in an attempt to reassure him.

Feeling agitated, she jumped up and walked over to the window to see if she could spot Charlie making his way back over to tidy up. The scene outside looked much the same, yet Katy had a nagging feeling that something was not quite right. What could it be?

Her fears were soon confirmed by Patrick, who joined her at the window. "Look at the cars, Katy. People don't drive cars like that anymore; cars like that are kept in museums."

Katy looked down the street at the cars. "They do look strange. What's going on? Maybe it's just an old car rally."

"But the gardens are different too," replied Patrick, sounding increasingly panicked. "Most of them had been paved over for parking cars, but look at them now. They look like vegetable gardens."

"You're right. But there must some reasonable – " began Katy nervously but Patrick cut her off.

"The street lamps are all wrong too, they look like gaslights." Patrick began to tremble with fear and reached out, gripping Katy's arm tightly.

A sinking feeling began to build in the pit of Katy's churning stomach as she took a moment to consider Patrick's observations. It was only then that she caught sight of the calendar on the wall. The page had previously said May 15th, 1942. Now it read April 12th, 1942. This date was also circled boldly in red. Katy stepped towards it in order to read the writing scrawled underneath.

Evacuees Katy and Patrick Parker arrive at station at six o'clock. Pick up.

Katy opened her mouth to speak but no words came out. She stared at her brother, frozen to the spot. What on earth had happened while they were asleep?

Chapter 4

What Next?

Katy reached out, pulling Patrick closer. She desperately wanted to leave the house but was terrified of what she might find outside. With no other option available, they both ran quickly to the front door and flung it open. Once outside, they paused for a moment to breathe, before running and stumbling down the garden path towards the front gate where they stopped once more. What would they do now? Where could they go?

Before they had time to consider any further, the garden gate swung open and through it burst a small girl, holding the hand of a breathless, fair-haired woman. Both looked familiar to Katy. An icy shiver ran down her back as she realised they were the people she had seen in Charlie's photograph – Mrs Graham and her daughter Susie. Mrs Graham looked older than she had in the portrait on the landing but it was definitely her. What was going on? How could they be here now? Living and breathing?

"Well, there you are!" said Mrs Graham, a large welcoming smile lighting up her face.

"You must be Katy and Patrick. I've just been to the station to collect you. This is my daughter, Susie. Say hello, Susie."

Susie smiled shyly, giving them a little wave. "I'm almost four. My birthday is next month," she whispered before swiftly hiding behind her mum's skirt. All that could be seen of her was a pair of enormous blue eyes peeking out at them, framed by a fluffy halo of white–blonde hair.

Katy and Patrick stared in stupefied silence, unable to respond. Katy's thoughts raced. Was it possible? Had they really travelled back in time to the 1940s? Katy stared at her brother and could see he was thinking the same thing. After a long pause, Patrick cleared his throat and stepped forward, holding out his hand to Mrs Graham.

"Yes. Hello. Sorry about that. Our train arrived early so we decided to make our own way here."

"Oh well, you're here now. As long as you're safe and sound that's all that matters. Where's your luggage?" inquired Mrs Graham.

"It's lost. We gave our bags to the porter at King's Cross and he loaded them into the luggage compartment but when we arrived at Knutsburry they'd disappeared," Katy said, surprising herself with her quick thinking.

She sighed with relief; all those old wartime films she'd watched with her mum would prove useful. At least she had *some* idea what life was like in the olden days.

Mrs Graham gave a long sigh and tutted. "It's not the first time. Don't worry; I've got plenty of spare clothes you can borrow until yours turn up. I expect you'll want to see your new room and settle in. Out you come, Susie," she said, pulling the small figure out from behind her skirts.

"Take Katy and Patrick up to their room. They can freshen up and get ready for tea. The twins will be back from cricket soon."

Staring at them curiously, Susie led Katy and Patrick into the hall and up the stairs. Everything looked exactly the same, except newer. The air was filled with the sweet perfume of roses, which stood in jugs and vases on every available surface. The slightly stale smell had disappeared. Susie led them to the back bedroom which overlooked the garden – the same one they had dressed up in earlier that afternoon. Once she had shown them their room, Susie retreated, smiling shyly before running back downstairs to her mum. Katy shut the bedroom door firmly and sank down onto the nearest bed, speaking to Patrick in an urgent whisper.

"What's going on? This is crazy. It's impossible! I just can't believe it. What are we going to do?"

Patrick lay comfortably on the next bed with a huge grin on his face. He was no longer scared and was looking as if he was starting to enjoy every minute.

"This is awesome, Katy! We've gone back in time! I mean, I've read about this sort of thing happening in my science fiction magazines – they call it a rip in time. The idea is that you pass through it either into the future or the past but I didn't think it could happen in real life. Brilliant!"

Katy looked at him in total disbelief. "What do you mean 'brilliant'? We're stuck in the past! Mum will be worried sick! How on earth will we get back?"

Patrick sat up and rested his head in his hands, staring silently into space, clearly giving the matter some serious consideration. Finally he spoke up. "We've just got to go along with it, play our parts as evacuees until we can work out how to reverse whatever's happened. It'll be exciting! There's a war on after all. I bet you'll get an excellent mark for your project when you hand it in with all this first-hand knowledge you're getting."

Katy was speechless. She stared at her brother in complete disbelief. Further conversation was cut short by the voice of Mrs Graham calling up the stairs to them. *"Katy! Patrick! Come downstairs. The twins are home – tea is on the table."*

Taking a deep breath, Katy pulled open the bedroom door and slowly walked downstairs. Patrick followed behind, whistling chirpily.

In the centre of the kitchen stood a large pine table, which had been covered with a white cloth and set for tea. At the table sat two twin boys who were about twelve years old. Both had thick, wavy, blonde hair, tanned faces smothered with freckles and small, round glasses. They wore white, hand-knitted V-necked cricket jumpers with shirts underneath. They both waved as Katy and Patrick entered the kitchen, introducing themselves as Frank and Harry.

Mrs Graham sat at one end of the table, pouring out cups of tea. At the other end sat Susie on a high stool, singing *Humpty Dumpty* loudly, happily entertaining the others. Frank, obligingly tumbling dramatically off his stool at the appropriate moment, made everyone burst into fits of laughter.

"That's enough silliness, Frank. Susie, please be quiet. What will Katy and Patrick think of us? It's like a zoo in here," said Mrs Graham.

Susie stopped singing and sat sulkily, her bottom lip jutting out. Frank picked himself up off the floor, brushed himself down and sat back up at the table, grinning.

"There's space here next to Susie for you, Katy. Patrick, you're next to Harry," instructed Mrs Graham, as she cut thick slices from a loaf of homemade brown bread.

"We're having eggs from our chickens," said Susie excitedly, picking up an egg and almost dropping it.

"Poppy laid this one. She's my favourite. Mummy's cutting soldiers for me to dip into my yoke. Do you want them too?"

Frank interrupted, "Mum has even got out the fruit cake in your honour. She's been saving it for weeks."

Katy looked at the table and her heart sank. This wasn't the sort of food she was used to eating and she didn't think she was going to like it. *I'm going to starve here*, she thought to herself as she looked at the brown bread and fruitcake.

The twins were used to the endless round of evacuees coming to stay and asked a hundred and one questions, some of which were tricky for Katy and Patrick to answer on the spot.

"What's your story then?" asked Frank. "Every evacuee has one."

Katy looked at Patrick, unsure of what to say. Katy was shocked to see Patrick winking back at her. He quickly threw himself into the role of 1940s schoolboy. Katy noticed that he'd even picked up the old-fashioned style of speech, saying things like, "Gosh! This cake is super!" and, "This homemade bread is spiffing!" At this point Katy almost choked on her food and needed thumping on the back several times by Harry.

Patrick didn't seem stuck for something to say, as he launched into a fantastical tale of their recent past. "Our Dad is an admiral in the Royal Navy.

Frightfully important. Involved in some hush-hush, top-secret operation. Mum disappeared rather mysteriously. She speaks several languages, including French and German. We think she's working as an undercover spy and has been parachuted behind enemy lines to make contact with some important agents."

Katy couldn't help giggling at the thought of her librarian mum as a daring spy. She shot Patrick a warning look and gave him a swift kick under the table in an attempt to shut him up. Unstoppable, he launched into another tale, describing in elaborate detail his own daring escape from Paris, just before it fell to the Nazis and how he fled to freedom by crossing the channel in a rowing boat, whilst being pursued by the enemy. Katy caught the twins exchanging incredulous looks, so decided now was the time to butt in.

"Ignore Patrick, he's got an over-active imagination. He's well known for exaggeration. Our real story is not nearly so exciting. Our mum and dad are involved in some boring routine war work and thought it would be safer to have us out of the way for a while. So here we are."

Luckily a knock at the back door stopped the twins from asking anymore tricky questions.

"Come in," called out Mrs Graham, and in walked another young boy who was slightly older, aged around fourteen. He was tall, with jet-black hair and large, bright blue eyes. He was dressed in cricket whites like the twins and carrying a bat under his arm. He smiled at the group and leant over to tickle Susie, who, judging by her giggles and smiles, clearly adored him. Both Katy and Patrick instantly felt that they had seen him before – those twinkling, bright blue eyes were so familiar. Puzzled, they stared at him, trying to figure out why he looked so familiar.

It all became clear when Mrs Graham said, "Sit down Charlie. Help yourself to some bread. Meet Katy and Patrick, our latest evacuees." She turned to Katy with a smile on her face, "Charlie usually turns up just as I'm putting food on the table."

Charlie laughed good-naturedly and pulled up a chair next to Susie, whilst helping himself to bread. "Hello, you two. You've landed on your feet at Willow Dene with Mrs Graham. She always puts on a good spread at teatime, even with rationing making things so difficult."

"That's enough, Charlie. We're just lucky to have all this space. It means we can grow our own veg and keep a few animals. Most aren't so fortunate."

"Don't forget the bees," said Frank.

"Mum has got two hives at the bottom of the garden. The honey comes in very handy as there's never enough sugar."

"Like I said, you've landed on your feet here," said Charlie.

As everyone helped themselves to more tea, the conversation around the table turned to the War and the whereabouts of Dr Graham.

"Read Daddy's letter again, Mummy. Please," pleaded Susie.

Mrs Graham sighed as she reached across to the mantelpiece above the fire, taking down what looked like a well-read and much-loved letter. She began to read it aloud, with the children joining in with their favourite bits.

"Love to all my precious children, be good and help your mother. Your loving father."

"Right, you heard him," said Mrs Graham, a sadness flitting momentarily across her face, before disappearing behind a brave smile. "Harry, you're washing up. Katy and Patrick, you can dry. Everyone does their bit here."

"Come on, Susie. I'll read you a story," said Charlie, picking up Susie and swinging her round and round till she squealed for him to stop.

* * * *

At half past seven that evening, Mrs Graham put down her knitting. "Come on, Charlie, off you go, anyone would think you haven't got a home to go to. Tomorrow is a big day for Katy and Patrick; they'll both be starting at their new schools."

Patrick sat up, yawning and rubbing his eyes. "I am rather tired you know. Train journeys always have that effect on me," he said, with a sly glance at Katy.

Katy, however, felt rather alarmed by Mrs Graham's comment. "You can't mean we'll be going to different schools in the morning?"

"Of course, dear. Patrick will be at St Joseph's, with the twins and Charlie, and you will be at the sister school, St Hilda's."

"Don't worry," said Charlie. "I'll call for you both in the morning at half past eight and we can all walk to school together. St Jo's and St Hilda's are on the same site, so you'll be close to each other."

Mrs Graham shooed Charlie out of the back door, then turned to Katy and Patrick. "You'll both need a bath tonight. The twins will show you where everything's kept and I've laid out nightclothes on your beds. I'll be up with your new school uniforms soon."

Reluctantly, Katy turned to make her way up the stairs. As she did so, she felt a small hand slip into her own and squeeze it tightly. She looked down and saw Susie, smiling up at her. "We can be sisters," Susie whispered quietly to Katy.

"I'd like that," replied Katy. "Come on; I'll read you a story while Patrick is in the bath."

Katy was touched. She'd often dreamt of having a little sister instead of an annoying little brother. Happily, she cuddled up with Susie to read a well-thumbed copy of Cinderella.

Going to bed in 1942 wasn't straightforward. Instead of a long, lingering soak under a power shower, Katy and Patrick had to have a bath. This wouldn't have been so bad if they had been allowed to fill it up to the brim with lots of hot water and bubbles but apparently this was forbidden. Frank had drawn a thick black line all around the bath at a height of five inches and had warned them sternly not to fill the bath above it.

"Is that all we can have?" said Katy to Patrick in shock, "it won't even cover my knees!"

Patrick washed first, and then called Katy into the bathroom. "I've saved the water for you but it's getting cold, so you'd better be quick."

"No way!" screeched Katy, horrified. "I'm not using your dirty water."

Just as she was pulling out the plug, Frank walked in and stopped her. "What do you think you're doing?" he asked shaking his head in disbelief and firmly putting the plug back in. "Warm water is a valuable resource – you can't just waste it! Don't you know that? Now hurry up, Susie needs to get in next."

Katy locked the bathroom door and reluctantly climbed into the now tepid bath. As she suspected, the water didn't even cover her knees and the carbolic soap smelled terrible too – just like tar! To top it all off, the bathroom felt cold and there didn't appear to be any form of heating. After the quickest bath in the history of baths, she returned to her room to find Mrs Graham waiting, her arms full of an assortment of old clothing.

"Let's try these on for size. You first, Patrick."

Patrick had to wear short grey trousers with grey knee length socks, a white shirt with a school tie and a green, hand knitted jumper, all topped off with a green school cap.

Patrick tried on everything enthusiastically. "Thanks, Mrs Graham, this is great."

Mrs Graham patted him affectionately on the head, ruffling his hair and smiling at him. Katy, on the other hand, shot him a scathing look.

"Your turn, Katy. Stand up and let's see if this fits."

Katy stared in absolute horror at the outfit Mrs Graham held up to her.

"You've got to be joking!" she exclaimed. "That's my new uniform? I can't wear that!"

Her new uniform had the same pea-green colour as her modern day one, but now consisted of a pleated, knee-length pinafore dress, accompanied by a white blouse with a large, round collar and knee length dark green socks. A straw boater with a green ribbon tied around it completed the look.

"Don't be silly, Katy, it's a lovely uniform and quite modern too. The green will suit your colouring.

Besides, lots of children would be grateful for good, clean clothes like these."

Patrick laughed and Katy stuck her tongue out at him. Mrs Graham tutted at them both.

"That's you two sorted. Here are your nightclothes. Lights out in twenty minutes. I'll be back to say goodnight shortly."

Patrick seemed happy enough in a pair of old-fashioned looking blue and white striped pyjamas. Katy gingerly picked up a long, white, cotton nightie with capped sleeves. Hiding from Patrick behind the wardrobe door, she quickly pulled it on.

"I look like someone's gran in this!" whined Katy miserably, as she looked in the mirror, longing for her usual fleecy pyjamas.

Patrick looked up from a pile of comics the twins had lent him and sniggered. "It's not like anyone you know is going to see you. I don't know why you're bothered," he replied.

Katy glowered at him and resentfully got into bed, picking up the copy of *The Twins at St Clare's* by Enid Blyton that Mrs Graham had given her to read. It looked a bit childish but she might as well give it a go. If nothing else, it might give her an idea of what to expect at school in the morning. Katy opened the book and was touched to see Mrs Graham had written in the front:

To Katy, I hope you enjoy this and your time at Willow Dene. Best wishes, Mrs Graham.

Katy tried to concentrate but found it impossible. She still felt worried about the whole situation and she missed her mum and dad. She wasn't surprised at missing her dad – he was always travelling for work and she was almost used to missing him now. But missing her mum surprised her somewhat, as all they seemed to do lately was argue. If she ever got back home she vowed she'd try harder to be a better daughter. *Please don't leave me stranded in 1942*, thought Katy to herself.

Deep in thought, the next twenty minutes flew by and, in what seemed like seconds, Mrs Graham had returned to say goodnight. She leant over and kissed them both on the cheek, stopping to give Katy an affectionate squeeze on the shoulder. At once, Katy felt tearful. It had been years since she'd had a goodnight kiss. She remembered when she was younger, both her mum and dad would come upstairs to tuck her in and say goodnight. She would lie in bed, listening to the sounds of them bustling around in the kitchen. Music from the radio and their muffled conversations would drift up the stairs. But since her dad had started travelling so much for work, things had changed.

Mrs Graham turned out the light as she left the room. Filled with dread and unable to stop worrying about what tomorrow held in store, Katy tried to get comfortable but even the bed felt different. There were no comfy quilts here but sheets tucked in tightly, with a scratchy blanket on top. Now the light was out, the room was plunged into darkness. Katy remembered learning about the blackout and special curtains in history lessons. It looked nothing like night-time at home, where all the streetlights meant it never became truly dark.

Patrick whispered through the darkness to Katy, "You OK? You seem a bit upset."

"Well that's hardly surprising, given the circumstances. I think 'upset' would be considered normal by most people. But then you're not most people," Katy huffed in annoyance.

Ignoring Katy's temper, Patrick continued, "What do you think of the twins? How weird is it meeting the younger version of Charlie? It's so strange – I love it! I wonder what's going to happen next. I can't wait to find out."

Forgetting her annoyance, Katy found herself replying, "Well, the twins seem nice but I want to tell them that I've got a letter from them in the future and that they live in Filey."

"Well don't say anything yet," urged Patrick. "They'll just think you've lost the plot! We can't prove anything – no one will believe our story. We can't risk being sent away from Willow Dene. It's our only link with our future."

"I hate to admit it, but I think you're right," replied Katy sullenly. "We'll just have to play along until we can figure this thing out. Do you agree?"

Silence.

"Patrick," hissed Katy but no reply came.

Typical, thought Katy to herself. *He's fallen fast asleep, as if this sort of thing happens to him all the time! I bet I lie awake all night.*

Yawning heavily, she closed her eyes and rolled onto her tummy, thoughts of what tomorrow might bring looming large.

Chapter 5

Old School

A strange noise woke Katy early the next morning and for a few moments she panicked, unsure of where she was. Slowly, the events of the previous day came flooding back as she looked around the unfamiliar bedroom. Her stomach sank; it hadn't just been a bad dream.

What on earth was that terrible noise? Katy quietly crept out of bed and tiptoed over to the window. Pulling the thick blackout curtains to one side, she peered nervously out. In the distance, at the bottom of the garden, she spied a hen house. Upon the roof stood a large cockerel, crowing loudly. It must have still been early as no sound came from anywhere else in the house. Looking at her watch, Katy saw it was still only five o'clock in the morning. Relieved, she crawled back under the covers, pulling them over her head. She lay there thinking of all that had happened since yesterday morning.

She must have fallen back to sleep as the next thing she knew, Susie was jumping up and down on her bed. "Wake up, Katy, breakfast is ready. Mummy says you need to hurry up."

Rubbing her eyes, Katy sat up, stretched and then did a double take when she caught sight of Susie, who appeared to have been in the dressing-up box already. She wore what looked like one of her mum's frilly nighties, with several long necklaces around her neck; her lips and cheeks were smeared with red lipstick. Over her shoulder hung a small, black, beaded handbag.

Katy suppressed a giggle and said, "Don't you look lovely this morning, Susie. But aren't you a bit overdressed for breakfast?"

Susie threw her a comical look, replying in a haughty tone, "Mummy says a lady must always look her best."

Katy burst out laughing as she pulled herself out of bed, casting an eye over her uniform hanging up on the wardrobe door. "That'll be hard for me in this outfit. It's horrible."

"I think it's lovely," sighed Susie, trying on the hat and doing a twirl. "I wish I could go to school with you."

Looking over at Patrick's empty bed, Katy began wondering where he was and why he hadn't bothered to wake her up. "Have you seen Patrick this morning?"

"Yes, he's playing soldiers with the twins; they wouldn't let me join in. I hate boys," she replied, frowning and stamping her foot.

Katy smiled, "Don't worry, I'll play dolls with you later if you like."

Susie's face lit up into a huge smile as she lunged forward, giving Katy a big hug, then skipping out of the room, humming yet another nursery rhyme.

"What was all that about?" asked Patrick, appearing in the doorway, already dressed in his new school uniform and looking every bit the 1940s schoolboy.

"Oh, nothing. Susie is just feeling a bit left out. Why didn't you wake me up?"

"I tried but you just pushed me away and pulled the covers up over your head. I could hear the twins, so decided to see what they were up to. They're a great laugh."

Suddenly, Mrs Graham's voice called out to them from the kitchen, *"Katy, Patrick, hurry up! Breakfast is nearly ready."*

Katy groaned. Some things never changed it seemed, whatever decade you found yourself in!

After a quick wash in the freezing cold bathroom, Katy returned to her bedroom to find the uniform laid out for her, with the addition of what looked like a pair of absolutely enormous navy-blue knickers. They were so big they actually had a pocket on one of the legs! Reluctantly, Katy got dressed and was horrified to discover that the legs of the knickers almost reached down to her knees. Her heart plummeted as she looked at herself in the mirror. She was unrecognisable. Picking up the old, brown, leather satchel Mrs Graham had given her for school, she headed downstairs to join Patrick and the others for breakfast.

Everyone else was already sitting around the kitchen table, waiting for Mrs Graham to ladle porridge from an enormous saucepan into their bowls.

"Morning Katy, I hope you slept well." Mrs Graham greeted her warmly.

Susie looked up at Katy with a smile and pulled out the seat for her. Katy took a bowl of porridge. "Is there any sugar?" she asked.

"We haven't had any sugar for weeks now," moaned Harry. "Use this instead," he said, pushing a sticky jar of honey across the table towards her. After the porridge they ate homemade brown bread, with margarine and marmalade. Mrs Graham picked up a jug of milk and poured a glass for Katy, who immediately took a large gulp and then gagged. The taste was unexpected – warm, sour and slightly cheesy.

"That's horrible," she choked, promptly spitting the milk back into her glass.

The twins laughed. "Don't you like our Emily's milk, then? Frank got up extra early to milk her so you'd have some fresh for breakfast," laughed Harry.

Katy was wondering who Emily could be and why they were drinking her horrible milk, when Mrs Graham chipped in. "Leave her alone, she's just not used to goat's milk that's all. She'll soon get used to it or go without. No one can afford to be fussy when there's a war on."

Breakfast continued at a much slower pace than either Katy or Patrick was used to. The twins kept everyone entertained with an endless stream of stories about school, all of which seemed to involve some near death scenario at the hands of the school bully, who was aptly named Brutus. At home they usually ate breakfast on the go. Katy quite liked how everyone sat down together – it helped take her mind off the coming day.

It can't possibly be any worse than normal school can it? thought Katy.

Her worries were interrupted by Mrs Graham, who placed brown paper packages in front of her and Patrick. Patrick ripped his open excitedly to find a toy soldier – just like the ones he had been playing with earlier with the twins. "Thanks Mrs Graham, this is great!"

Mrs Graham smiled at Patrick and then turned to Katy. "It must be difficult for a girl of your age being away from her mum. I thought you might like this to write in, like a diary. You can record your experiences of life as an evacuee, and perhaps show your children one day."

Opening the package, Katy found an expensive-looking, red, leather-bound journal.

"Thanks, that's a great idea," said Katy, "I'll keep it with me all the time."

You never know, she thought, *it might come in handy, if I ever do get home and manage to finish my project.*

A moment later, she heard a knock on the door and, without waiting to be invited, in walked Charlie, still munching a half-eaten piece of toast. "Come on you four, you'd better get a move on. It's old Higgins on gate duty. He'll give us a black mark if we're late. One more this term and I'll get six of the best."

"What do you mean?" asked Katy, hoping Charlie wasn't about to say what she suspected.

"The cane, you nitwit, what do you think I mean?" said Charlie. "You'd better be careful," he said, turning to Patrick, "they're quick to dish out the punishments at St Joseph's for all sorts of things."

"Like what?" Patrick asked nervously.

"Messy work, ink smudges, dirty nails, hair touching your collar. Talking in class will get you a hard rap of the ruler across your knuckles. If a master thinks you're insolent he won't think twice about caning you and asking questions later."

Patrick gulped. "I can't believe your teachers are actually allowed to hit you." Both Patrick and Katy had learned about this sort of punishment in their history lessons but being here and knowing that it could possibly happen to them made it feel a lot more serious.

The twins laughed. "What sort of school have you been going to then? Our school motto is 'Spare the rod, spoil the child'. Our headmaster, Mr Cooper, takes it very seriously. He likes to have flogged at least four juniors before he breaks for his elevenses."

Patrick looked really quite worried. Charlie pushed the twins aside and said, "Shut up, you two. It's not so bad. Keep your head down, follow the rules and you'll be fine. It's just that the twins are trouble makers, always up to no good."

"What's my school like?" asked Katy, nervously.

"The nuns are fierce – so watch out – especially for Mother Superior. Just don't catch her eye. Last week Tilly Burton was made to kneel all morning for passing notes in class."

Katy was horrified – she and Lizzie were always passing notes in class. If they were ever caught, the worst that ever happened to them was detention!

Harry laughed at Katy's horrified look, then added, "Usually it's just ritual humiliation, designed to take you down a peg or two. You know, being made to stand in the corner with the dunce's hat on. It'll be the making of you. At least, that's what they say."

"Ignore the twins," interrupted Charlie. "It's not so bad. Most of the meanest masters have gone off to fight. They've been replaced by some really elderly types. And St Hilda's can't be that bad. There are only a few nuns left and my cousin Hillary worships a couple of them. It's Sister Mary this, Sister Maria that. You can ask her yourself. She's meeting us outside the school gates to take you to your classroom."

Katy shot Patrick a nervous look at the mention of Hillary. What would a teenage Hillary be like? All Katy could picture was a very sad, slightly spooky old lady.

Feeling completely overwhelmed, Katy began to panic. Taking a deep breath, she dug her nails into the palms of her hands, desperately trying to stop herself from having a total meltdown in front of everyone. She needed to be on her own while she tried to get a grip. Fighting back the tears, she escaped into the front room and stood gazing out of the window. Her feelings of panic were quickly replaced by confusion. Katy could see a scruffy young boy, aged about seven, and carrying a shovel almost as big as himself, traipsing behind a coal cart, which was being pulled by an enormous shire horse. Unbelievably, he seemed to be collecting horse droppings from the road and putting them into a large metal bucket.

"Why is he doing that?" asked Katy out loud to herself, with a look of disgust on her face.

Mrs Graham popped her ahead around the door, "Whatever's wrong Katy?" she asked following Katy's gaze out of the window, then throwing back her head and laughing out loud. "You're a funny girl, Katy. It's as if you're from another world. Haven't you seen anyone collecting horse dung before?"

Katy shook her head and looked at Mrs Graham in disbelief and grimaced.

"But what does he want with horse poo?"

"Manure of course! It's the best to be had," exclaimed Mrs Graham. "Marvellous stuff – does wonders for the vegetables. You've seen my roses, haven't you? They're absolute beauties."

Winking, she nudged Katy, saying, "Your turn next. You'll find the shovel outside the back door."

You won't catch me picking up poo, thought Katy.

"You'd better get a move on. Don't forget your gas mask; it's hanging behind your bedroom door. Don't worry, Katy, everything will be just dandy," said Mrs Graham, giving Katy's shoulder a gentle squeeze.

Susie insisted on walking with Katy down the garden path, holding onto her hand tightly and then stood waving till they turned the corner and finally disappeared out of sight.

The walk to school felt surprisingly familiar. Not a great deal had changed except for the obvious lack of modern cars, although the streets were just as busy with old-fashioned cars and horses and carts. All too soon, they arrived at the front gates of St Hilda's and St Joseph's. Everything looked much the same, except the front lawns had been dug up and made into a large vegetable garden. The huge staff car park now housed several bikes, an assortment of animals and yet another chicken house.

A large, black, forbidding sign read, 'Girls' Entrance', and next to it another said, 'Boys' Entrance'. It looked as if Katy and Patrick would have to say goodbye for the day. Leaning against the gate stood a short, plump girl with a chin-length chestnut bob, hazel eyes and a broad smile on her face.

Katy stared at her in amazement. It couldn't be, could it? Her suspicions were immediately confirmed as the girl leant forward holding out her hand in greeting.

"Hello. I'm Hillary and you must be Katy. Its jolly nice to meet you but we must hurry. The bell is about to ring any minute. If we're late for assembly we've had it. Stick with me today and you'll be fine, I promise."

Unbelievable! thought Katy, feeling stunned, utterly unable to connect this young, smiling girl with the Hillary she had feared for most of her childhood.

Patrick and Katy said a hurried goodbye as both were whisked off in opposite directions. Hillary linked arms with Katy and began hurrying her up the stairs and in through the imposing main entrance. Luckily they were able to slip into the back of the school hall unnoticed, joining the other pupils who sat silently in neat rows, waiting for the dreaded Mother Superior to arrive. They had made it just in time. Mere seconds later, a piano began playing and on cue the girls stood up and began to sing, *All things bright and beautiful.* That was Katy's dad's favourite hymn. She felt close to tears as she realised how much she missed him. She couldn't even remember the last time she'd really talked to him. When she was little, he used to play with her for hours, making up all sorts of games. But work was taking up all of his time now and everything had changed.

Assembly seemed to drag on for hours. Mother Superior looked very stern in her voluminous black habit. Her pointed features protruding from her tightly bound headdress, reminded Katy of a large crow. Tall and painfully thin she walked with a slight stoop, and on her feet she wore sensible, flat, black lace-ups. Perched on the end of her pointy nose balanced small, round glasses with metal frames.

I can't imagine how she is meant to inspire us girls onto great things – she looks terrifying, thought Katy.

Mother Superior spent most of the assembly reminding the girls of their duty to King and country. Katy listened, spellbound, to the seemingly endless list of clubs and activities that the girls were expected to join in with. When did they get to just muck about and relax?

"Don't forget girls, the knitting club meets today in room six. Miss Strauther will be demonstrating how to knit socks for our brave boys overseas. Tomorrow at one o'clock the gardening club will harvest the new potatoes with Sister Maria. Meet outside the greenhouse at half past twelve sharp. Finally, please remember everyone is required to attend the St John's Ambulance first aid training on Friday after school at four o'clock. It is imperative you learn basic first aid procedures in case we ever have an incident."

She means in case we ever get bombed, thought Katy.

On the wall at the front of the assembly hall, Katy could see an enormous map of Europe, with various coloured flags pinned onto it. Mother Superior finished her assembly by telling them about the latest war campaigns whilst moving a couple of flags around. Finally, they all said the school prayer and were dismissed to their classrooms to begin the day's lessons.

"Come on, Katy, this way. Our classroom is 9B. It's a bit of a maze around here, but you'll soon get used to it."

Classroom 9B felt familiar to Katy as it had once been her form room. It soon became apparent that the St Hilda's Katy knew in the future hadn't spent a great deal of money on modernisation. It was practically unchanged, except for a few minor differences such as tape across the windows. Katy knew from her history lessons that this prevented the glass shattering during a bomb blast.

Hillary introduced Katy to her teacher, Miss Dobson, "This is Katy, Miss. She's Mrs Graham's new evacuee."

Katy felt relieved to see that Miss Dobson was neither a nun nor very fierce looking. In fact, she looked very young and rather scared herself.

"Good morning, Katy, welcome to St Hilda's. I hope you'll be very happy here," said Miss Dobson in a gentle voice. "You can sit at the desk next to Hillary for today."

Hillary whispered to Katy, "She's only about twenty but she has to train on the job because of the shortage of teachers. She's a bit nervous." Hillary went on to describe Miss Dobson as 'a good egg', and a 'total sport' – both expressions made Katy giggle helplessly.

Pupils sat at individual wooden desks, which had lids that lifted up to reveal storage for books and pens. Writing was done with ink pens and the ink well on Katy's desk was full. *Oh help,* thought Katy, *I'm always in trouble for messy work when I use a normal gel pen.*

Katy followed Hillary's example by hanging her gas mask in its box on the back of her chair. Katy had tried hers on earlier and experienced the terrible smell of nasty rubber. It was difficult to breathe in, too. Katy hoped that she and Patrick would never have to wear one for long, especially as she had pointed out on the walk to school that Hitler had never used poisonous gas during the war. Charlie had looked puzzled when she said this. "How can you possibly know that?" he had asked in disbelief.

Much to her dismay, Katy quickly realised her abilities as a student were even worse in 1942 than in the present day. So far they had studied Latin and French grammar. Katy had been called upon twice to answer and each time had got it wrong. The rest of the class had smirked at her.

Soon, lunchtime arrived and Katy felt curious to see how the food would compare with the school lunches she was used to. It ought to be much worse she reckoned, what with rationing and all that. She imagined nettle soup and dried eggs and shuddered.

"Come on then, let's get to lunch. I'm starving," Katy called out to Hillary as she strode off purposefully in the direction of the school refectory.

"Hang on a minute," called out Hillary, rushing to keep up with her. "You seem to know your way around very well considering it's your first morning. Are you sure you haven't been here before?"

Oops, thought Katy as she casually replied, "No, I've just got a good sense of direction, that's all. Plus, I followed the crowd."

Hillary nodded. "There's a space at my table so we can sit together. Our table is quite good fun. It's a nice bunch of girls except for Morag and Laura. They're table monitors this term – worst luck."

"What are table monitors?" asked Katy. "We didn't have them at my old school."

"It's their job to get the food, bring it to the table and serve everyone. But you've got to watch them. They're very generous with servings when it's something horrible but ever so stingy if it's something they like, so that they can give themselves enormous helpings."

Katy followed Hillary into the school dining-hall. It looked very different from what she was used to. For a start, all the pupils had set places at certain tables. Each table seated ten girls and every table was laid, ready and waiting for the girls to eat. There were even tablecloths!

Just as Hilary had explained, the table monitors dished out everyone's meals. "What's this meat?" asked Katy, probing a grey, gristly lump with her fork. She had struggled to swallow her first mouthful.

The girls around the table laughed out loud. A tall, pretty, blonde girl answered, "Cook says it's beef mincemeat, but no one believes that. We reckon its cat!"

Hillary interrupted her, "Lots of cats have been disappearing in Knutsburry since rationing began."

Katy suddenly felt sick and pushed her plate away in disgust.

"What are you doing?" asked Hillary. "You can't waste food like that – you have to finish it."

Katy looked at her helplessly and slowly pulled her plate back, forcing down a few more mouthfuls of the mystery meat.

"Is pudding any better?" she asked hopefully as she finished her last bite. The girls giggled again.

"Pudding's just as bad. Wait and see," replied a serious-looking girl, who seemed to be squinting behind a pair of very thick glasses. The table monitors returned, plonking a large bowl unceremoniously in the centre of the table. Katy held out her bowl and a white, glutinous substance was spooned into it.

"Tapioca?" she asked uncertainly, looking at the unappetising mess in her bowl.

The girls smiled knowingly at one another and then chorused, "Frogspawn!"

Katy put down her spoon, trying to ignore the rumbling in her tummy.

"I'm not hungry anymore!"

Much to her relief, the girls spooned Katy's portion back into the large bowl and divided it amongst themselves.

When lunch was finally over, Mother Superior, who sat with all the other teachers on the long top-table, rang a small handbell and the whole hall fell silent. She stood up, made the sign of the cross and began a lengthy prayer. Only then were the pupils finally dismissed, table-by-table and allowed some free time.

"Follow me," said Hillary to Katy. "I'll take you to my favourite spot." She led Katy up the familiar path across the school field to the oak tree where Katy and Lizzie spent most of their lunchtimes. Hillary threw down her school bag, lay on the grass with her feet propped up on the trunk and proceeded to chat non-stop.

"Have you got any brothers or sisters?" Katy asked, finally getting a word in.

"Of course, I'm one of seven! Our Mark's the eldest. He's twenty-one and in the Royal Air Force," she replied proudly, pulling a photograph out of her inside blazer pocket and handing it to Katy.

"Mum's ever so worried about him, doesn't even breathe when she sees the telegram boy walking down our street. Always thinks it'll be bad news."

"Why's that?" asked Katy, without thinking.

Hillary gave her an odd look, "She thinks he'll have been shot down or is missing in action, of course."

"Oh, right," said Katy, feeling silly. "What about your dad, is he in the army?"

"No, Dad is too old; he's a baker in town. Mum works for him most mornings. She never usually does this but she slipped a little treat into my bag today. I think she felt bad for me after I described yesterday's lunch – unidentified meat with unidentified vegetables! She knows how bad the food is here. She came here herself in the dark ages."

Reaching into her school bag she pulled out two jam tarts. "Here, take this."

Katy polished it off in two greedy mouthfuls – far nicer than what was on offer for pudding!

Across the school wall, she could just about see into the boys' playground, where some of them were playing football. She hoped Patrick was getting on OK. She wished she could talk to him but the teachers patrolled the dividing wall, determined to prevent any fraternizing with the opposite sex.

The rest of the afternoon passed slowly and Katy felt exhausted when Miss Dobson finally rang the hand bell on her desk and dismissed them for the day. Hurrying to the school gate with Hillary, she found Patrick, Charlie and the twins waiting for her. As the six of them walked home together, Katy found herself making a mental note of all the subtle changes she saw, determined to record them in her journal later. That way, if she ever did get back home, she could use it as research.

As they walked home, Katy noticed more differences that she didn't understand. "Where have all the street signs gone?" she asked.

The twins looked at her as if she were mad. "They took them all down. It's meant to confuse the enemy if they ever invade. Mind you, I don't know what the Nazis would want with sleepy old Knutsburry," Charlie laughed.

"And why do I keep seeing kids going into the corner shop with empty bottles?" she asked.

More bewildered looks followed this question. "Don't you know anything?" said Frank. "Where have you been living for the last couple of years? Mars? Glass is scarce now so if you want to buy a drink like Dandelion and Burdock you take in an empty bottle and they fill it up from the barrel."

The High Street, too, was very different. All the chains Katy knew had disappeared and in their place were individual shops: a baker, a butcher, a fishmonger and something called an ironmonger, all in a row. There were also far fewer cafés and restaurants.

* * * *

That night, as she sat up in bed, Katy carefully made notes in her journal of everything she had seen. She even drew a map of the High Street as it was in 1942, labelling it carefully. Next, she wrote down all she had to eat that day. Pleased with her efforts, she shut the book and carefully placed it back into her satchel, switched off the light and lay down, listening to Patrick's rhythmic breathing as he slept.

Immediately, her thoughts turned to Hillary. In just one day she had grown fond of her – she was so friendly and funny. Katy hated knowing what an awful future awaited her and wished desperately she could warn her of what lay in store. But Patrick had been adamant that she couldn't tell Hillary anything. Feeling frustrated, Katy pulled the covers up over her head and sighed wearily.

Fingers crossed, she made a wish, hoping with all her heart that she could somehow save Hillary from her awful fate and that one day soon she'd be back home in her own bedroom, showing her journal to Lizzie as a prized souvenir from a very strange adventure.

Chapter 6

Friend or Foe?

Sunday arrived and Katy realised with some surprise that they had completed a full week in 1942. After supper, Charlie called round and they all lounged on the floor in the parlour, listening to their favourite radio programme. Afterwards, Charlie got out a pack of cards and they played a game called 'Chase the Ace'.

They were just beginning another game, when they became aware of the now familiar sound of enemy aircraft flying overhead. Katy and Patrick had quickly learnt to recognise the droning noise that the bombers made as they passed over Knutsburry on their way to bomb the Liverpool docks.

"Come on, quick," shouted the twins, leaping up and racing to the attic stairs to get a better view of the action. At first this ritual had scared Katy and Patrick. They were afraid a bomb would be dropped on Willow Dene by a passing plane. But Charlie had quickly reassured them, saying, "Nothing worth bombing in Knutsburry. Most exciting thing to happen here was when a German plane dropped loads of leaflets saying we should surrender – that an invasion was imminent."

They watched from the attic window in excited silence as the sky above Liverpool blazed with light. Brilliant white flashes from anti–aircraft fire lit up the night sky like a Christmas tree, filling it with an eerie orange glow. Suddenly, the sound of the aircraft changed.

"What's that? Listen you lot. Shush," called out Charlie urgently.

From their vantage point the children could see a plane; it seemed to be faltering, losing speed and height. It had clearly been left behind the rest of its squadron.

"It's coming down – look! I don't believe it," shouted Frank in amazement. Charlie and Harry both cheered, going wild with excitement. Patrick and Katy looked at each other, unsure of how to react.

"What's that? Can you see it?" shouted Charlie. "It's an airman! He's parachuted out!"

They watched in astonishment, as the man seemed to float gently down to earth, like a descending angel of doom. Next, they heard a distant thud, as the aircraft hit the ground in a nearby field. The children stood staring at one another in a stupefied silence.

Quickly, Charlie sprang into action. "They've come down in Mossop's field! If we take the shortcut through the woods we can get to them before anyone else arrives. I bet we'll find some cracking souvenirs to trade at school!"

"We could take the pilot prisoner and hand him to the police," agreed Frank

"Let's do it," cried Charlie and Harry in unison. "We'll be heroes!"

"But what about Mrs Graham," said Katy nervously. The last thing she wanted to do was upset Mrs Graham after she'd been so kind to them. "Won't she worry if she finds we're all gone?"

"Don't worry about Mum – she's giving Susie a bath and putting her to bed. A routine that's taking longer and longer since you've arrived Katy! She doesn't like going to bed while we're all still up – she thinks she's missing out on fun. Mum will be busy with her for ages – she won't even notice we're gone!"

They headed back down from the attic, stopping at the storeroom to collect a torch and some rope with which to tie up their prisoner.

"Come on, Katy!" moaned the boys impatiently, as they stood nervously outside the back door. Katy hurried over to them, shutting her satchel and flinging it over her shoulder.

"What are you bringing that for?" asked Patrick, puzzled.

"Wait and see," Katy whispered mysteriously, patting her bag.

"Come on, we'll have to run for it or we'll miss our chance," called Charlie.

The moon shone brightly, lighting their way and making their progress to Mossop's field quicker than expected. At the edge of the field they slowed down and then stopped dead, unsure of how to proceed. Their hearts pounded as if they were straining to get out of their chests.

"There it is, look at it! It's a beauty," said Harry, as he shone the torch in the direction of the plane, now mostly shrouded in shadows. It was nose down and had lost a wing in the crash. A warm orange glow could be seen coming from the cockpit, which must have caught fire on impact.

"Right, listen to me," said Charlie, taking charge. "I'm the eldest so I'm responsible for you lot. You have to do what I say, OK?"

Everyone seemed to accept this and nodded to one another silently. The reality of what they were about to do suddenly hit them. They were happy to have Charlie take control. Things seemed a lot scarier than they had in the attic at Willow Dene.

"We need to be very quiet. The pilot might be armed and things could get nasty. Stay in my shadow until we know for sure."

The mood of anticipation and excitement had been replaced with a growing feeling of nervous tension, which seemed to pulsate on the night air all around them. Katy's breathing became shallow and rapid as she clutched her bag tightly to her chest. She followed the others, cautiously making their way over to the plane.

Holding their breath they moved close enough to peer inside the burning cockpit.

"Quick, let's take a look around and see what we can find as a souvenir," whispered Harry.

"Look at that – its blood!" gasped Patrick, pointing to a trail of thick, deep, crimson droplets smeared on the outside of the window and onto the pilot's seat.

"He's wounded – his parachute must be around here somewhere. He can't have gone far. Stick close together. Let's find him," Charlie instructed.

Shining the torch onto the ground so they could pick out the trail of blood, Charlie led the way. It was easy. The pilot must have been bleeding quite heavily.

"Shush, listen. What's that?" asked Patrick.

A low moaning and whimpering sound carried gently on the night breeze. It reminded Katy of a trapped, injured animal and she winced at the thought.

"It must be the airman," said Patrick. "It's coming from over there. Come on, follow me."

Following the sound along the edge of the field, they arrived at an old broken-down cowshed and approached its entrance nervously.

Will he put up a fight? What if he has a gun? Questions raced through Katy's head.

Cautiously, they shone a beam of light into the shed. Nothing could be seen except for a few bits of broken machinery and straw bales. Katy let out a loud sigh of relief. "Well that's it then – he's got away. Let's get home before we're missed."

"Hang on a minute, give me that torch," said Patrick urgently. "Look, what's that in the far corner?"

Shining the torchlight in that direction they were able to make out the outline of a body, crouched down low with some sort of sacking thrown over it. As they watched, it jerked and a gentle low moan came from within.

Without thinking Katy rushed forward, flinging off the sacking to reveal the cowering figure of a young man. He looked up at Katy with such fear and pain in his eyes that she felt a sob escape from her own lips. Almost immediately, she was pushed out of the way by Charlie and the twins, who grabbed the airman and attempted to tie him up with their rope. He put up no resistance, gasping out in pain as they pushed and pulled him from side to side.

Something inside Katy snapped and she could bear it no longer. "Stop it, stop it now! You're hurting him – he's injured. He's no threat to us."

The boys looked at her in disbelief. "Why do you care? He's a Nazi – he's the enemy. We never should have brought a silly girl with us," snapped Harry angrily.

But Katy was powerless to stop herself. "He's only a boy himself. He can't be more than twenty. He's just doing his job. Just like Hillary's brother, Mark. If Mark's plane went down over Germany you'd hope whoever found him showed him some kindness, wouldn't you?"

Sensing their hesitation, she seized her chance, pushing them aside and crouching down low. "Where do you hurt?" she asked slowly and gently.

With difficulty he pulled open his jacket to reveal a badly injured arm. His uniform was soaked in blood and Katy flinched at the sight of it. Gritting her teeth, she reached into her satchel and pulled out Mrs Graham's first-aid kit. Taking some cotton wool, a small bottle of witch hazel and a long bandage she tenderly began to clean and dress the wound. Thank goodness she had joined the St John's Ambulance training at school with Hillary. At least now she had some idea of what to do.

"Here, drink this," she said holding a small bottle of brandy carefully to his lips so he could take a sip.

"You're for it now, Katy," exclaimed Frank in dismay. "Mum's been saving that for the Christmas pudding."

"Oh shut up! He needs it to help numb the pain," replied Katy angrily, before turning her attention back to the pilot and helping him to drink.

"What's your name? I'm Katy and this is my brother Patrick. That's Charlie, and I'm sure you can tell that these two are twins – Frank and Harry."

"Jan. My name is Jan. Thank you, thank you for your kindness," he replied in almost perfect English. "Please, tell me, have you seen my crew? My navigator and gunner bailed out several fields back but I waited until certain I wouldn't crash into any homes."

The boys looked at each other wide-eyed with fear, anxious that they might suddenly be surrounded by a hostile enemy. Patrick swallowed hard, then spoke up, "No we haven't seen any one else nearby."

Jan gave Patrick a weak smile of thanks. "Don't be scared. I won't hurt you." Exhausted and obviously in great pain, he closed his eyes but held on tightly to Katy's hand.

"Just in time," said Patrick, as they heard the roar of engines. Jan opened his eyes. Letting go of Katy's hand he fumbled around in his inner breast pocket, pulling out a crumpled black and white photo with a name and address written on the back. "Please help me, I beg you. These are my parents, Isla and Ivan Dieter. Let them know I am safe, otherwise they will think the worst. They have already lost my two brothers in this war. It will destroy them to receive a telegram saying I'm missing in action, presumed dead."

Katy quickly took the photo, slipping it into her satchel, and promised to let them know as soon as she could. The very next minute the cowshed was full of soldiers and the children were pushed to one side. Jan was firmly escorted to an army truck and whisked away.

After a long stern lecture about how dangerous their interference had been, the children were driven home to Willow Dene by a young corporal.

"Don't tell our mum, please," begged the twins. "Our dad is away. You'll just upset her. We won't do anything like this again. We promise, sir."

The corporal looked at them, clearly considering their plea. Katy had one last try, "Please sir, we just wanted to do our bit for the war effort. We feel so useless, just being kids. We thought this was our chance to really make a difference, instead of just knitting socks."

The truck pulled up at the end of their road, out of sight of Willow Dene. "Go on then, get out before I change my mind – but keep out of trouble, do you hear? Next time you might not be so lucky." The children clambered out of the truck and, without a backward glance, the corporal sped off back to camp.

They let out a collective sigh of relief and wearily walked back to the house, pausing briefly at the gate to say goodbye to Charlie.

"Wow! Wait till we tell them at school tomorrow. They'll never believe this!" cheered Frank as they made their way up the garden path.

"But that's just the problem," said Harry, "They won't believe us. We don't have any proof."

"That's where you're wrong," said Patrick, a huge grin on his face. With a flourish he pulled out a small knapsack from under his coat. "I think you'll find all the evidence we need in here. I spotted it behind a hay bale and managed to grab it when no one was looking. It belongs to the pilot. It's got his logbook in it, some German chocolate and what looks like a lucky charm!

Smiling at one another, the children sneaked back into the kitchen and sat around the kitchen table to carry on their game of cards and not a minute too soon, as Mrs Graham shortly appeared in the doorway.

"Good gracious! Are you lot still up? It's time everyone went to bed. And I don't want any arguments. I've had a hard enough time putting Susie to bed tonight!" she laughed.

Katy tried to protest that it was far too early but Mrs Graham simply tutted and said, "Growing children need their sleep. But first, you need your supplements. Line up, please."

Katy and Patrick looked at one another puzzled, wondering what on earth she meant, whilst Frank and Harry groaned out loud. "Do we have to, Mum? We eat well. We don't need supplements."

Mrs Graham ignored the twins and stood before them, holding out a large tablespoonful of thick, golden liquid. She beckoned Katy forward. "Open up nice and wide dear. This cod liver oil will keep you healthy and regular."

Katy held her nose and swallowed. It tasted awful! Next, came a spoonful of something called malt, which was surprisingly nice. Once everyone had been given their supplements, it was time for bed.

Katy got into bed and took out a pen and the writing paper that Mrs Graham had given them to write to their parents. She began to draft a letter to Jan's parents in Germany.

"What if they can't read English?" asked Patrick.

"They're bound to," replied Katy. "Jan's fluent. If not, someone will translate it for them. How should I start?"

"Well, remember its 1942 so it'll need to be formal, you know, old fashioned. You don't want to scare them so just stick to the facts.

Katy began to write,

Dear Mr and Mrs Dieter,

My name is Katy Parker. I am writing to you on behalf of your son, Jan. You have probably been told he is missing in action but do not be alarmed. He is safe and well. His plane crashed into a field near to where I live, in the town of Knutsburry, Cheshire. A group of us found him sheltering in an old barn and looked after him until the authorities arrived and took him away. We were told that he will be kept as a prisoner of war at the local camp and be put to work on a nearby farm, where he will be well looked after.

Best wishes,
Katy Parker

Chapter 7

Settling In

The next couple of weeks passed by in a blur; Katy and Patrick soon settled into their new routine. Every morning, Susie woke Katy up, usually by jumping vigorously up and down on her bed. Then they all began their chores. Life in 1942 was much more regimented than either Katy or Patrick had been used to. It was a real shock to the system having to be up every morning by half six at the latest. It seemed everyone had jobs to do; even Susie had to lay the table for breakfast.

It was Katy's job to feed the hens and collect any eggs that had been laid during the night.

Susie loved the hens and had a name for each one. Whilst Katy cleaned out their coop, Susie would sing songs to them, believing this made them lay more eggs.

Just after breakfast Charlie would appear, and they all walked to school together. Once school was over, they played out on the street with a gang of kids until Mrs Graham called them in for supper. Then it was homework, a radio show and bed by half eight! Katy had found this hard to believe at first, but in a strange way had almost started to enjoy it.

'Nit Night' came as the biggest surprise of all. At first Katy hadn't understood what was going on.

"Come on Katy, you're first," called Mrs Graham from the kitchen. Katy wandered into the kitchen expecting to be told to dry the dishes. Mrs Graham was laying a large piece of shiny, brown paper over the kitchen table.

"Sit down and lean your head over the paper."

Katy looked confused. "But why?"

"I need to check for nits, of course. Now let's see what we can find, shall we?"

Mrs Graham began to comb Katy's hair carefully over the paper, as she looked for nits.

Once Katy and Patrick were safely in bed with the door shut, they shared stories about their school day.

"It was brilliant, today. Not like school at all. I worked with Charlie in the school garden, digging vegetable beds and collecting new potatoes for the kitchen. He's sort of the head gardener for the school, the real one got called up and there was no one left to replace him. He says he dreams of cabbages," reported Patrick, happily. He seemed to be enjoying his time in the 1940s.

"That sounds like Charlie," said Katy smiling.

"After lunch we had Mr Anderson for English; he must be at least eighty. You won't believe this but he actually fell asleep in class and sat snoring behind his newspaper! His glasses were perched on the end of his nose and whenever he did a particularly loud snore they almost fell off. Then he'd jerk himself awake, smile at us all, mutter, 'Well done boys, that's the spirit,' and fall back to sleep! It was hilarious. We played cards and read comics all afternoon!"

Katy smiled to herself and said, "Sounds more fun than my day. We did French and Latin all morning, then needlework this afternoon. Only Hillary makes it bearable. I hope her brother Mark is going to be OK. I keep thinking about the golden memorial plaques in the hall at school."

Patrick looked puzzled, until Katy reminded him, "You know, the ones that commemorate all the former pupils who died in the war."

"Do you think his name is there? You can't tell Hillary," urged Patrick.

"That's just it, I've read them loads of times but I can't remember if his name is there or not. It makes me feel sick to think it might be. I'm glad Charlie is here. It seems safer with him around," said Katy.

"I know, I'm glad he's here too," replied Patrick. "It feels like nothing really bad can happen while he's around."

"Do you think we should tell him? You know, about us and what's happened?" said Katy.

Patrick thought for a while then replied, "Better leave it for a bit, see if we can really trust him. It's a bit of a mad story for anyone to believe after all."

Katy felt lost. What were they going to do? How would they ever make it home? They had been at Willow Dene for weeks now and there still was no clear sign of what they were supposed to be doing there or how they might get back home.

Tears welled in her eyes as it all suddenly became too much for her. "We're never going to get out of here, Patrick. I just want to go home," she sobbed.

Patrick was silent for a moment, staring at his sister who seemed to be falling apart at the seams. He took a deep breath. "Maybe you're right. Maybe we should tell Charlie. What have we got left to lose?"

Katy looked up, puffy eyed and through her broken sobs said, "Do you think so? We'll have to time it right."

"Let's wait until we know him a bit better," said Patrick, taking over as the older sibling and comforting Katy. "Once we've gained his trust a bit more, we can tell him."

"And hopefully he won't think we're insane," said Katy and they smiled at each other.

With that decided, they both rolled over, exhausted, and quickly fell asleep.

* * * *

On Saturday morning, Katy stretched lazily: enjoying the extra few minutes in bed, feeling refreshed and rested after yet another good night's sleep. It was weird but the nightmares had completely stopped. She hadn't had a single one since their arrival in 1942. Katy shuddered at the mere thought of them. Fingers crossed, they'd gone for good.

Saturday was definitely the best day of the week in her opinion. It was the one day of the week they were allowed to sleep in till half past seven.

"You awake yet, Katy?" whispered Patrick.

"I am now," said Katy grumpily. "I miss my lazy Saturdays, sleeping till lunchtime. But we'd better get moving or we'll be late for the film. The queue was massive last week – it went halfway down the street! I can't believe so many kids are at the cinema by half past nine in the morning."

"What are we seeing? I liked that cowboy film last week," replied Patrick.

"Frank said it's the usual cartoons first and then it's the new Disney film. Guess what it is? Dumbo!"

Patrick laughed out loud. "It's weird to think it's just been released. I didn't know it was so old!"

"I know! Remember us all watching it that Christmas ages ago? You couldn't stop crying," giggled Katy.

"Shut up, it's a sad film – you cried too," said Patrick, picking up his pillow and throwing it at her. "And remember Katy, don't give away the plot. You've got to act like it's the first time you've seen it. You keep slipping up: talking about things you shouldn't know."

"I'll try. What time is Charlie calling for us?"

"Just after nine so we'd better get moving!"

* * * *

After the breakfast dishes had been cleared away and the jobs done, Mrs Graham shooed them out of the house on the understanding that they would not return before one o'clock for lunch. Even with a war on, kids seemed to have more freedom in the 1940s.

Soon, Katy and Patrick had been living at Willow Dene in 1942 for almost a whole month. On their fourth Sunday evening, they once again sat up in bed, trying to figure out what they were meant to do and why they had been sent here. Patrick felt certain they would return to their future when they had completed whatever task or mission they had been sent to complete. He seemed quite confident about this and Katy discovered a newfound respect for him.

He was no longer an annoying little brother to be avoided or teased but almost like a friend. How weird to like Patrick – whatever next?

Katy felt certain the answer was staring them in the face but they couldn't see it. What could it be?

Chapter 8

The Answer

Katy lay awake that night, desperate to figure out why they had been sent there and how they could get home. What could it possibly be? She racked her brains and stared into the darkness.

Suddenly, it was as if a bolt of lightning struck her. It was so obvious she couldn't believe it had taken her a month to work it out. Brimming over with both excitement and fear she crept quietly out of bed, desperate to wake Patrick and share her idea. Gently shaking him by the shoulder, she whispered urgently in his ear, "Patrick, wake up, it's important. I've figured this thing out once and for all."

Patrick sat up yawning and rubbing his eyes. "This better be good, Katy. I'm tired. I was having a lovely dream," he mumbled, still half asleep.

"It's the bomb! That's why we've been sent here. I remember Charlie saying the one and only bomb that ever fell on Knutsburry fell on 15th May, 1942! It's obvious, isn't it – we're meant to stop it happening and save everyone."

Patrick was suddenly very awake. "But how? We can't change the course of history. We don't know what will happen if we do."

"What do you mean we can't change history? Who's going to stop us?" challenged Katy.

"I mean we shouldn't. It's dangerous to mess about with fixed dates in time. If we change things, we might alter the whole course of history for the worse – it's called the butterfly effect," said Patrick.

"You've been watching too much TV. Your theories are wrong Patrick – we have to change it. I'm going to save Mrs Graham and Susie. Are you going to help me or not?"

"Calm down, Katy. Think about it. No one is going to believe us if we try to warn them about the bomb. Everyone is always saying that it's a quiet war around here, that Hitler would never bomb sleepy old Knutsburry. I don't see how we can make a difference."

"Today is the 12th of May. We have exactly three days to work this thing out and come up with a plan."

Neither of them had a clue how to proceed but before Patrick could reply the door creaked open and Mrs Graham popped her head around. "Quiet you two. Katy, get back into bed and no more chatting, it's very late. The twins have been asleep for ages. Sweet dreams and I'll see you both bright and early in the morning."

The urgency of the situation was confirmed first thing the next morning when the twins didn't appear for breakfast.

Mrs Graham walked downstairs with a worried look on her face. "Keep away from the twins. They're covered in chickenpox and feel quite poorly with it. I've covered them in calamine lotion to stop the itching and told them to stay in bed. You'll have to do without their company for a couple of days, I'm afraid."

Katy looked at Patrick. It had started – just as Charlie had described to them that day in his garden. What could they do?

Willow Dene felt unnaturally quiet without the twins crashing about and jumping out of cupboards to scare you. No tennis balls or cricket bats lay around the corner waiting to trip you up. Even the usual routine of school had been interrupted by the start of the May halfterm holidays.

They spent Monday morning doing jobs for Mrs Graham, who was expecting some new evacuees from Liverpool called Doris and Edna Burton. Katy was stunned when she heard Mrs Graham talking about the possibility of Doris and Edna being sent to Canada by boat to escape the war entirely and live with distant relatives.

"But how will they see their mum and dad?" asked Katy.

"Doris and Edna have been very unlucky. Their mum was killed a couple of weeks ago in an explosion at the munitions factory where she worked. They've been staying with various neighbours ever since."

"But what about their dad?" asked Katy.

"He was killed at Dunkirk, trying to rescue soldiers from the beach. There are no living relatives left in England that can give them a proper home. That's why they're coming to us, just until it's all sorted out."

For the first time, the harsh reality of the war really hit Katy. She and Patrick had been enjoying playing at it for the last few weeks but for everyone else around them it was a grim reality.

"I'll help out as much as I can, Mrs Graham, just let me know what I can do," Katy whispered in reply, a sudden sadness falling over her at the thought of Doris and Edna's misfortune.

"Well, I do have something in mind. I wasn't going to tell you, as I wanted it to be a surprise but with the twins being ill, I'll need an extra pair of hands. The Parish Council has arranged a special treat for evacuees and their host families."

"Ooh, what's going to happen?" asked Katy, excitedly.

"We're having a party in the village hall in the afternoon," answered Mrs Graham, "and then we're going to the cinema to see some cartoons. There's a lot to do, what with decorating the hall and getting together enough rations to make a cake and sandwiches. Lots of people are contributing so we should be able to put on a good spread."

Katy and Patrick were kept busy for the next two days making bunting and banners to decorate the hall and helping out. As a result they had got no further in working out how to evacuate the cinema before the bomb fell. Sitting at one of the trestle tables in the village hall, making paper chains, they quietly discussed their options.

"Charlie said the bomb fell early in the evening, around six o'clock. We've got to time our plan right. But what can we do?" whispered Katy.

"Why don't we just go to the cinema with everyone. Just before six o'clock we could create a disturbance – shouting and screaming that everyone's got to leave because a bomb is going to fall on the cinema," suggested Patrick.

"That won't work. No one will believe us. They'll just think we're causing trouble, trying to spoil things. We'll be the only ones made to leave the cinema," said Katy.

"You're probably right. We need to do it so everyone automatically starts to evacuate without questioning it," he replied.

"But how? I keep racking my brain, but I can't come up with anything. . . I think it's time we talked to Charlie. I'm certain that's what we're meant to do. I just hope we haven't left it too late. In the meantime, let's try and persuade Mrs Graham not to go to the cinema – we have to at least try something."

* * * *

On Wednesday morning, Katy and Patrick woke early, consumed by mounting dread and anxiety. They both felt sick to the pit of their stomachs with the thought of what would happen later that day.

In the kitchen, Mrs Graham was busy making up a breakfast tray for the twins with boiled-eggs and soldiers. "As soon as you've both had breakfast and done your chores, I want you to go back up to the village hall and help with the sandwiches and tidying up, please."

"I want Katy to stay and play mums and dads with me," demanded Susie. "It's not fair; I never get to do anything good. Why can't I come to the cinema with you?"

"I've already told you, Susie, the film starts too late for you. Katy will take you on Saturday morning," replied Mrs Graham.

As planned, Patrick and Katy took the opportunity to try and dissuade Mrs Graham from going to the cinema. "Do you think it's a good idea to take Doris and Edna to the cinema this evening? They'll probably be tired after all their travelling and want an early night," said Patrick.

Mrs Graham considered this briefly, then dismissed it. "Oh no, they'll enjoy it. They need a distraction after all they've gone through. They can have a lie in tomorrow morning."

It was Katy's turn to try and change her mind. "The twins seem much worse this morning, I'm not sure you should leave them this evening. What if they need you and you're out?"

"Stop worrying you two. Everything will be fine. Hillary is coming round at five o'clock to babysit Susie and keep an eye on the twins. She's more than capable of dealing with any problems. Enough of this nonsense, we still have lots to do if we're going to be ready for the party at two o'clock."

Katy and Patrick set off for the village hall, a feeling of impending doom hanging in the air around them. They were greeted at the door by Mrs Evans, the vicar's wife. "I'm glad to see you two!" she exclaimed, looking rather red-faced and flustered. "There's still so much to do. Katy you're needed in the kitchen to help prepare the sandwiches. Patrick, Charlie is in the store room and needs help with the chairs."

Katy made her way to the kitchen, which had become a hive of activity and noise. Someone had set up a gramophone on the serving hatch and lively old-fashioned dance music played as they all worked together in a sort of production line, trying to get things ready in time for the evacuees' arrival. Someone passed her an apron and thrust a large bowl of hard-boiled eggs into her hands, instructing her to peel and mash them for egg and cress sandwiches.

The next couple of hours passed in a whirl of excitement as the finishing touches were put to the village hall. It was a large wooden building with windows all down one side, and a raised platform at the far end, on which amateur drama productions and music concerts took place. On the far wall hung a large portrait of the King and Queen and several Union Jack flags. A long row of wooden trestle tables had been set up down the centre of the room and they had been covered with a wide variety of different coloured tablecloths that had been donated especially for the occasion.

"You three can skedaddle now," said Mrs Evans, "You'll need to go home and get ready for the party. The room looks lovely – you've all done a great job. Make sure you're back here in time to greet the evacuees. We want them to feel welcome."

"Katy," hissed Patrick urgently, "we have to tell Charlie now. We can't put it off any longer."

Katy felt sick with anxiety. "We'll tell him on the walk home. . . What if he can't help us?"

The three of them wandered off back home, walking slowly and chatting as they went. A lull in the conversation gave Patrick the courage to spit it out, once and for all. "Charlie, we have something to tell you. It's not a joke. We're deadly serious. In fact it's a matter of life and death that you believe us."

Charlie stopped walking and turned to face Patrick. "What's this then Patrick? You sound a bit scared."

Patrick glanced at Katy, his eyes full of worry. Katy picked up the story for him. "This sounds crazy Charlie. . . but something terrible is going to happen tonight just after six o'clock."

Charlie stared at them both, "What do you mean, something terrible?" he asked.

Katy took a deep breath and continued, "A German bomber is going to drop a bomb on Knutsburry. The bomb is going to land on the cinema and kill everyone inside. We need your help, Charlie. We can't stop the bomb falling, but we can try and keep everyone safe. We just need to come up with a plan."

Charlie stared at them with an incredulous look on his face. After a long pause he finally said, "That's not a very nice joke. Bombs are no laughing matter. You should know that, being evacuees from London."

Katy replied, "That's just the thing Charlie. We're not actually evacuees at all. Not really."

"What do you mean you're not evacuees? You're not making sense Katy."

"I'll try and explain if you'll just listen, Charlie. It won't be easy to believe but please try."

Charlie stared at them both and folded his arms, signalling Katy to carry on. Katy hesitated. Charlie didn't look like he was going to believe them. With no other option, she launched into their tale – one she had silently rehearsed many times. The sense of relief she felt at finally being able to share their story with someone else was overwhelming.

"Patrick and I are really from the future. We were spending the afternoon at Willow Dene, researching life during the Second World War for my history project."

Patrick interrupted, "We had just eaten a lovely tea prepared by you!"

"What do you mean, prepared by me? Have you both gone mad?" said Charlie, scornfully.

"No Charlie, it's true. We know you in the future. You look after Willow Dene for the twins. Your grandson, Tom, goes to our school – Katy's got a crush on him!"

Katy elbowed Patrick. "Stick to the important facts. We'd been listening to the radio and reading old magazines and we both fell asleep. When we woke up, we found ourselves in 1942."

Patrick interrupted once more. "It's taken us a while to figure it out but we finally know why this has happened. We've been sent here to save the people in the cinema, especially Mrs Graham and Susie. They're not meant to die – not yet – not like this."

Charlie sat down with his head in his hands. After what seemed like an eternity, he looked up at them both with a look of complete disbelief on his face.

"Can you prove any of this? You can't just expect me to believe a story like this without proof."

Katy and Patrick stared at each other helplessly. Proof? They had nothing; Charlie would never believe them now.

Suddenly, Patrick jumped up and screamed out in delight, "I *do* have proof for you! When I met you in the future we chatted in your potting shed. You showed me your granddad's medal. He'd survived the trenches of the Great War and gave you the medal for luck. You promised your granddad you'd carry it with you always. Go on put your hand in your pocket, I bet it's there!"

Charlie stared at Patrick in astonishment as he pulled the medal out of his pocket, just as Patrick had said.

"How did you know that? I haven't told anyone that Granddad gave me that medal. . . I can't believe I'm going to say this but. . . I think I believe you. There's no way you could know about my medal unless I told you."

Charlie then became very excited and full of questions about life in the future. Katy was trying her best to answer them when Patrick finally cut in. "There's no time for chatting, you two. What are we going to do about the bomb? We've got to save Mrs Graham and Susie. Susie is only three years old. We have to make sure she makes it to her fourth birthday next week."

Charlie sat lost in thought. Finally he looked up, smiling hesitantly, "OK, you two. I've got a plan. Listen up and I'll tell you what we can do."

The three of them huddled together and Katy and Patrick listened as Charlie hatched his plan.

Chapter 9

The Plan Unfolds

"You two go to the party. Then, at about half past four, start complaining that you feel ill and a bit itchy. I bet Mrs Graham will send you straight home to bed in case you're coming down with chickenpox, like the twins."

"That's a good idea," said Patrick. "We'll pretend to be really disappointed to miss out on all the fun."

"But what about Hillary? We've got to stop her babysitting. She blames herself for what happened to Susie in the future. Her whole life was affected by it," said Katy worriedly.

"But how will we stop her? Her mum won't want her to let Mrs Graham down and she's saving up for a bike so she needs the money," replied Charlie.

"And if she isn't babysitting, she'll be in the cinema and so not exactly safe! Besides, we're going to save Susie so Hilary will have nothing to blame herself for," Patrick added with a determined look on his face.

"Exactly. We'll just have to forget about Hillary for now until we work out the rest of the plan," instructed Charlie. "As far as I can see, her future depends on us evacuating the cinema before the bomb drops and Mrs Graham getting home in time to stop Susie disappearing."

"But how are we going to do that?" asked Katy, a frown etched onto her face whilst she nervously bit her thumbnail.

"The only thing that I can think of that will guarantee everyone leaves the cinema immediately, is to set off the fire alarm. No one will ignore that," replied Charlie with more confidence than he really felt.

"But how will we get into the cinema and set off the alarm without being stopped?" Katy asked, anxiously.

"That's the tricky part," said Charlie. "But I have an idea. Mr Mulligan will be working on the box office tonight with his son, Michael. Patrick and I will create a disturbance outside the cinema that will distract them away from the main entrance. Then, Katy, you can slip in unnoticed."

"But how will we create a disturbance?" asked Patrick, looking scared.

"I know," replied Katy. "Patrick, you collapse just outside the entrance, clutching your tummy, moaning and groaning, and pretending to be in terrible pain. Charlie can rush into the cinema to get Mr Mulligan's help and ask Michael to go for the doctor. He can say he's too scared to leave you."

"Brilliant. That will leave the way clear for you to slip into the cinema and set off the fire alarm. Then you can join the crowd of people leaving the cinema. No one will be any the wiser."

"Then, I'll make a miraculous recovery and we can all scarper," said Patrick, tying up their plan nicely.

* * * *

The afternoon was a great success and everyone seemed to have loads of fun – especially doing the treasure hunt that Patrick had organised. The prize was a copy of a book called *Peter and the Wanderlust*, donated by the school governors. A vast amount of food had been donated, too, and so, for the first time in years, the evacuees enjoyed an unlimited amount to eat instead of being told to save some for the next day.

When everyone sat down at the long trestle tables for tea, Patrick and Katy joined them but were careful not to eat much. Mrs Graham noticed at once that they weren't tucking in along with everyone else. "What's the matter?" she asked in a concerned voice, whilst placing her hand on Katy's forehead to check her temperature.

Katy replied weakly, "I don't feel well. My body aches all over and my head is pounding."

Patrick joined in at this point. "Me too. I feel itchy as well. I want to scratch all over."

Mrs Graham looked at the pair in concern. "You do feel a little hot. We'd better not take any chances. It might be chickenpox. Go straight home and get yourselves into bed."

"Oh no! Do we really have to leave?" whined Patrick. "I was really looking forward to the cinema!"

"Me too," said Katy in a weak voice. "It's so unfair!"

"Now, now, you two. I want to see brave faces, please. Off you go, home to bed. We can't risk over forty evacuees coming down with the chickenpox next week!"

Putting on their best miserable faces, Katy and Patrick said their goodbyes and set off for home. Once they were safely outside the hall, Katy turned to Patrick, the strain showing on her face. "Phew, that went well. Let's hope everything else goes according to plan!"

Back at Willow Dene, they went straight up to their bedroom, putting their nightclothes on over what they were already wearing in order to make a speedy exit once Hillary had been in to check on them.

"Katy, I'm scared," whispered Patrick. "What if we mess up and everything goes wrong?"

"I know. I feel the same. I feel sick at the thought of it all. But we mustn't think about failure. We *will* succeed Patrick. We don't have any alternative." Katy hoped she sounded more confident than she felt. At least Patrick seemed reassured but secretly Katy wasn't so sure they could carry off their plan.

They had arranged to meet Charlie at the back of the cinema at exactly half past five. Charlie wanted to go over their plan one last time and make sure everyone was clear on their role.

Just after five, Hillary stuck her head around Katy and Patrick's bedroom door to check on them. Katy and Patrick lay still and pretended to be asleep. Hillary played nurse, feeling their foreheads and tucking them in before quietly shutting the bedroom door. Katy and Patrick lay listening to her footsteps as she went downstairs. They heard her enter the kitchen, quietly shutting the door behind her and telling Susie to hush.

With the coast clear, Katy and Patrick jumped out of bed, quickly shedding their nightclothes and putting on their shoes.

"Here goes," said Katy. "Look, I've got Jan's good luck charm, the one we found in his rucksack. Here, touch it for good luck."

Patrick reached out and held the little silver pixie gently in his hand. He handed it back to Katy who stowed it away in her satchel, which she flung over her back. Very quietly, they made their way downstairs and out of the front door. They took the twins' bikes and cycled as quickly as they could to their agreed meeting place, arriving panting and breathless to find Charlie nervously pacing up and down.

From their hiding place, they could hear the evacuees and their host families arriving and starting to queue outside the entrance of the cinema. They heard Mrs Graham's voice as she laughed at some joke or other. The doors to the cinema opened and everyone began to troop excitedly inside. Katy looked at her watch. It was now or never.

"Right. Let's get started," said Charlie, bravely.

All three stood up, staring intently at one another. Then, with fierce determination they parted – Charlie and Patrick towards the cinema entrance, Katy into the shadows just around the corner from the main doors.

Katy watched their plan unfold as she hid in the shadows. As Charlie and Patrick made their way towards the entrance, Katy saw Patrick clutch his stomach and groan loudly. When they reached the steps of the cinema he collapsed dramatically, falling to the floor and screaming out in pain. Within seconds, Mr Mulligan rushed outside to help.

Katy could hear everything from her hiding place. "What's happened lad, what's the matter?"

Patrick just cried and wailed in response. Charlie answered for him. "He's got a grumbling appendix. That's what the doctor called it. I think it must have burst or something terrible. He just collapsed. I don't know what to do. Help him, please!"

Katy watched as Mr Mulligan called out, "Michael! Michael! Come quickly! We need your help, lad."

Within seconds, Michael had appeared outside and his dad issued instructions. "Run to the doctor's surgery and tell him it's a burst appendix – be as quick as you can, lad."

Whilst this exchange was taking place, Katy seized her chance and quietly slipped past them into the building.

Katy's heart began to pound and her breathing became rapid as panic threatened to take hold of her. With her hand shaking, she opened the door to the dimly lit corridor where Charlie had told her the fire alarm was and silently slid inside. The others had played their part, now it was all down to her. The enormity of the situation suddenly hit her; countless lives were dependent on their plan succeeding.

Momentarily paralysed by fear, she stood listening to the cartoon playing – she could hear the sound of children's laughter.

Katy pulled herself back to reality, shook off her fear and made her way over to the alarm, which was a small bell protected by a glass cover. Attached to it hung a small metal hammer on a chain. Katy picked up the hammer, held her breath and silently hoped that this would work, before hitting the glass firmly. It shattered instantly and the alarm began to ring loudly. Finally, Katy allowed herself to breathe.

The change in atmosphere was immediate. The noise level began to rise, children cried and adults called out directions to their charges. Soon, all the emergency exits were flung open as people began to rush outside as fast as they could. Katy quickly joined the flood of people escaping outside. Her job was done and just in time by the sounds of things.

Almost immediately, the air raid siren began to wail and the noise of a bomber could be heard close overhead, shattering the calm of the early evening sky. The crowds of people outside the cinema stopped – staring up in disbelief at the sky. A surge of panic rippled through the crowd.

"Run! It's a bomber!" called the air raid warden. *"Take shelter now!"* he shouted. At once, everyone began to hurry, all united in their desperate need to reach safety in the nearest public shelter. Katy managed to track down Patrick. Just as she reached him, she caught a glimpse of Mrs Graham running back to the safety of Willow Dene and to her children.

"We did it Patrick, we really did it!" cried Katy, grabbing Patrick by the hands and swinging him round and round whilst the doctor looked on, astonished by Patrick's miraculous recovery.

"Where's Charlie?" she asked, realising that Patrick was now on his own.

"His mum ran past this way and spotted him – she dragged him away with her. He tried to get me to go, too, but I had to wait for you. Katy, we have to get out of here."

Katy's excitement at saving Mrs Graham soon faded as throngs of people ran past her, all shouting. Patrick was right. They had to get to safety quickly, before the bomb dropped. They ran to the twins' bikes, which they had left behind the cinema.

"Head for Willow Dene and the cellar as fast as you can. We should just make it. Don't look back

Patrick and pedal as fast as you can," Katy called out as they fled towards the bikes. Katy leant down and picked hers up, jumping onto the seat in one swift movement. Her feet slipped off the pedals in her rush but she quickly righted herself and peddled furiously ahead.

She turned and shouted back at Patrick, *"Hurry up! Faster! Follow me!"*

A flash of blinding white light filled the sky, accompanied by a mighty roar and blistering heat. Katy lifted her hands to cover her face. She felt herself lifted up off the bike and propelled through the air before falling, down, down into the void below. It was then that she heard the voice, calling her name,

"K-a-a-a-t-y!"

All at once the pieces of the puzzle fell into place. Katy realised with an awful certainty that she was living her dream. This was the very moment she'd experienced night after night. The voice calling out her name was Patrick's. As Katy braced for impact, one thought whirled around her mind; *how does the dream end?*

Chapter 10

Reunion

Eyes tightly shut, fists clenched and with the roar of the blast still ringing in her ears, Katy felt the road, cold and rough beneath her cheek. She opened her eyes, slowly sat up and looked around. To her great relief, Patrick lay sprawled out on the pavement next to her. The early evening sky was bright blue. All seemed peaceful. Calm even. Not as if a bomb had just exploded nearby.

"We're back, Katy! We're back! We did it! We're home!"

Katy stared at Patrick with a dazed expression on her face, unable to take in what he was saying.

"Look around you. Look at the cars, the satellite dishes on the houses!" He picked himself up off the pavement and stood up. Slowly, Katy began to take in her surroundings. The relief she had felt moments ago suddenly vanished. "But what happened? Did we save them? Did they survive?" she choked on the words, tears welling in her eyes.

Before Patrick could answer, a voice called out their names. They both turned to see Charlie's grandson, Tom, running down the street towards them. Katy's heart missed a beat as she looked up and straight into his eyes.

"You two alright? I tried to stop you but you just cycled straight into the road works. It was like you couldn't see them or me!"

"Yeah, we're OK. We were just having a race," answered Patrick quickly. "We didn't hear you call out."

Katy stood up, feeling shaken, and gingerly brushed herself down. She saw with no surprise that she had a nasty graze all down her left leg and arm. She could also feel blood trickling down her cheek. Patrick had a nasty cut on his right leg and elbow.

"You two need to be more careful – look at you, you're both covered in cuts. Come on, I'll take you to my granddad's house. It's nearby. He'll clean you up. He learnt all sorts of first aid at school during the war."

Katy and Patrick followed Tom in a daze, slowly pushing their bent and twisted bikes. As they passed Willow Dene, Tom waved to a young couple who were busy trimming the high hedge at the front of the house. Katy noticed the large front door had changed colour. It was no longer bright red but was now painted a buttercup yellow. A small girl sat on the grass watching them. Her hair was tied in two bunches with ribbons that matched her bright red pinafore dress. She looked so incredibly like Susie that a sob caught in Katy's throat and she had to blink back tears. *What happened to her*, wondered Katy to herself.

"Who are they?" she asked.

"Steph and Laurence Graham," replied Tom. "They moved in just before Christmas. And that's their daughter Madeline. They were given the house by Steph's twin uncles, Frank and Harry. My Granddad Charlie used to play with them when he was a kid."

Patrick leant over and whispered in Katy's ear. "See, it's like I told you; our actions have had consequences. Things aren't the same as they used to be. I just hope we haven't caused loads of trouble."

They arrived at Charlie's house and Tom rushed straight into the hall, calling out, *"Granddad, come here. My friends, Patrick and Katy have had an accident."*

Charlie appeared in the kitchen doorway, giving them both a nod of the head and a knowing smile. An enormous sense of relief washed over Katy. Charlie! He was OK! Behind the worn and lined old face they could see the young boy they now knew so well.

"What have you two been up to then? On second thoughts, I don't want to know. I've got some antiseptic cream and cotton wool here – you'll soon be as good as new. You first, Patrick."

Katy wandered into the hallway as Patrick followed Charlie into the kitchen. Noticing a new photograph on the side table, she picked it up for a closer look. It showed the Graham family, happily posing outside Willow Dene. As Katy looked more closely she noticed several significant changes. Little Susie wasn't so little anymore. In this photograph she looked more like seven or eight years old and the twins looked much more mature.

Katy turned over the photograph and saw, written in faded blue ink, May Bank Holiday, 1946.

Katy felt herself both welling up with tears and wanting to jump up and down in excitement. They had done it; the past had been rewritten!

Katy rushed back into the kitchen. "Charlie, what happened the night of the bomb?"

Charlie paused, looking pointedly at Katy and Patrick a large smile unfurling on his lips. "Best bit of luck we ever had that was. Just minutes before the bomb landed, the fire alarm in the cinema sounded. Everyone evacuated the building so that when it hit, the cinema was completely empty. There were only two casualties that evening.

"Two evacuees who had been staying with Mrs Graham went missing. They were last seen just before the blast, cycling furiously away from the cinema. Poor kids couldn't have made it. They must have been caught up in the explosion. No bodies were ever found so no one ever knew for sure what happened them. The war office declared they were missing, presumed dead."

And with that, he gave them a wink.

Katy and Patrick's faces broke into huge grins.

"What happened to Mrs Graham, did she make it back safely?" asked Katy.

"Further bit of luck that was. Just as she came round the corner of Victoria Avenue, she caught sight of Susie letting herself out of the front gate and heading off down the road towards the High Street. I dread to think what would have happened if she'd been any later getting back," said Charlie.

And with a twinkle in his eye he added, "The future might have been very different indeed."

Katy and Patrick both jumped up and threw their arms around Charlie, cheering with relief.

At that moment, Tom walked into the kitchen, a surprised look on his face. "Eh. . . Have you guys met before? Or am I missing something? Granddad, Mr Dobson is at the front door. He says you're expecting him."

"Show him in, Tom. He's right on time. Mind you, I wouldn't expect anything else from a master clock maker."

A tall and very elderly gentleman, with a shock of unruly white hair, walked into the kitchen. He was stooping slightly and leaning on a wooden stick. He smiled warmly at Katy and Patrick as if he knew them, grabbing their hands and shaking them enthusiastically. Katy and Patrick looked at each other uncertainly. Did they know him?

Katy suddenly saw Patrick break into a smile as he said, "I recognise you now. You live on our street! Our mum told us that you used to own the jewellers on the High Street."

Mr Dobson stepped forward, smiling, whilst reaching into his pocket to pull out two small, rectangular packages. "Please accept these gifts. I made them for you a long time ago, always hoping that one day I could give them to you in person. I was an enemy and a stranger but you showed me great kindness. Katy, I also have this for you."

He held out a letter that was brown and yellow with age. Katy took it from him. It felt brittle, yet it was clearly addressed to her. With trembling hands, she carefully opened it. She scanned the page quickly. Unbelievably it was a thank you letter from Mr and Mrs Dieter, dated July, 1942.

Katy looked up from the letter and stared at the man in front of her. "Jan, is it really you?" whispered Katy, not quite believing it could be true.

Jan propped his stick against the table and sat down heavily. "Yes, it's me! Not quite the young pilot you remember. I changed my last name to a more English sounding one after the war."

"But how come you're here?" blurted out Patrick, "Why aren't you in Germany?"

"I worked as a prisoner of war at a local farm. Charlie used to look in on me and check I was OK. We became good friends and he told me all about how you two ended up in Knutsburry. Later he introduced me to his cousin Hillary and we got quite friendly. After the war we married, bought a house in Knutsburry and started a family."

Katy let out a squeal of delight, jumping up and down. "Hillary's married with children!"

Jan smiled at Katy and continued. "This town has been very good to me. We had no reason to leave. I've been waiting for a very long time for two special people to turn up. I couldn't risk missing them, not when I had these to give them."

Katy and Patrick took the two packages that he held out, slowly opening them. Inside, they found two beautiful watches, the leather straps softened with age and the gold mellowed to a soft honey.

"Turn them over," instructed Jan.

Katy and Patrick both followed Jan's instructions and discovered inscriptions written on the back.

For kindness to a stranger – May, 1942.

Katy was overwhelmed with emotions. Stuck for words to express how she felt, she leant over and opened her satchel. "I have something belonging to you," she said, pulling out Jan's knapsack and handing it to him.

Jan took it, hands shaking, and opened it, amazed to see the contents again after so many years. He flicked through his old logbook, smiling, and then lingered on the picture of his mum and dad before passing the bag back.

"You keep it. But I'll keep the photo if you don't mind."

Katy pulled the charm she had stowed away out of her satchel. "Do you want to take this?"

"Keep it, Katy. I hope the pixie continues to bring you luck. It certainly helped me. It brought you two to me. And now it's brought you back home safely again."

"I'll keep it with me all the time, I promise," said Katy.

Katy turned her attention back to Jan's gift. She took off the old watch she had found in the cardigan pocket, its glass face now all cracked and smashed by her fall from the bike. As she slipped it into her pocket she noticed the time had stopped dead at precisely six o'clock when the bomb fell. She carefully put on the watch Jan had made her, lifting up her wrist for everyone to admire.

"How did you know we'd be here? Today of all days?" said Katy.

Charlie and Jan smiled at each other. "We've been meeting on the 15th May for years, in memory of the two brave evacuees that went missing on the night of the bombing," explained Jan. "Which reminds me."

Mr Dobson fumbled once more in his coat pocket and pulled out a pale pink envelope. "Hillary asked me to give you this."

Katy tore open the envelope. Inside was a card. Smiling, Katy read it silently.

Dear Katy,

I have so much to thank you for, not least for bringing Jan to me safe and sound. I would love to see you again. Please come to tea next Sunday at three o'clock, we have so much to catch up on. Bring Patrick and Charlie. It'll be the old gang back together again for the first time in so many years. Except this time some of us are a bit older!

With love,

Your dear friend,
Hillary
Xxx

* * * *

Katy and Patrick slowly walked home, too tired to feel really excited or to discuss what had just happened. It was hard to comprehend what they had just been through. They had been gone for over a month but time had stood still while they were away. It appeared as if only an hour of real time had passed since they had said goodbye to Lizzie and fallen asleep on the floor at Willow Dene.

Standing at the bottom of their garden path, they looked up at the familiar front door. "I thought we'd never get back. It's hard to believe we're finally home," said Katy.

"You do realise no one will ever believe us, Katy. It'll have to stay our secret."

The front door opened and their mum appeared. "What are you two doing standing down there? In you come – dinner is nearly ready and there's lots to do to get ready for the start of term in the morning."

Katy smiled at Patrick. *Nothing's changed here then,* she thought affectionately. Surprisingly, she found this was a relief. "We're coming, Mum," she called out. They walked up the garden path and back into the warmth of their own home. Katy looked around at their house. They had taken everything for granted before their journey – the phone, the TV. Without thinking she leant forward and gave her mum a kiss on the cheek.

"What was that for?" her mum asked, a pleased look on her face.

"Just happy to be home again."

"You're a funny one, Katy," said her mum, smiling and hugging Katy towards her. "You've only been out a few hours. Did you get any good pictures for your project? I see you're still dressed up."

"What project?" asked Katy, a puzzled look on her face.

Her mum gave her a suspicious look. "Your Home Front project on the war. I thought that's what you were doing this afternoon."

It had been so long since Katy had thought about her project that she'd forgotten all about it.

Patrick quickly jumped in. "She's just being silly, Mum. She got loads of really great stuff – good first-hand information. It really felt like we were back in the 1940s for a while." He winked at Katy.

"I think I'm going to have a quick bath before dinner," yawned Katy, suddenly feeling exhausted and desperate to change out of her 1940s clothing.

As she undressed, she found the old, broken watch in her pocket that Lizzie had insisted she had put on, all that time ago. It looked beyond repair to her but perhaps someone could fix it or use the parts. She didn't need it – not now she had Jan's beautiful watch to wear. On the landing her mum had placed a box full of odds and ends, to be taken to the charity shop. Katy took one last look at the watch and placed in the box.

After soaking in a very full bubble bath and enjoying her dinner, Katy lay on her bed, chatting nonstop on the phone to Lizzie. "It's great to talk to you Lizzie – you won't believe how much I've missed you!" said Katy.

"What do you mean you've missed me you daft thing? I spent most of the afternoon with you at Willow Dene! What did you get up to after I'd gone?"

"Oh nothing much really, just fell asleep reading some old magazines and listening to the radio. You didn't miss much," replied Katy. She realised she was going to have to be a lot more careful with what she said to people. Patrick was right after all – no one would believe them.

* * * *

The next morning was the first day of the new term. Unable to sleep, Katy got up earlier than usual, her stomach full of butterflies. She had a very important meeting at lunchtime. It was still hard to believe it was actually going to happen – she had to pinch herself to check she wasn't dreaming!

Just as they were leaving Charlie's house last night, Tom had pulled Katy aside and casually asked her if she would be around at lunchtime and did she want to meet up? Katy had been completely lost for words but had surprisingly managed to stutter, "yes" in reply. They had arranged to meet outside the lunch hall at one o'clock that day. With this happy thought in mind, Katy picked up the old leather satchel, flung it over her shoulder and headed for the bus stop, Patrick once again trailing behind.

The first lesson that morning was History and Mr Oakley would be collecting their completed projects on the Home Front. Katy sighed with dismay. Lizzie had texted Katy that morning to say she was ill and wouldn't be in school. With all the rush and daydreaming about her rendezvous with Tom, she had forgotten to pick up the interviews they had done from Lizzie on her way in. They would almost certainly fail – and there wasn't a hope they'd win the competition. Lizzie was going to be furious with Katy.

Just then, someone walked past Katy's desk and accidently kicked over her satchel. Out fell the journal that Mrs Graham had given her to write in, and Jan's logbook!

Of course! thought Katy. She picked them up and handed them in to Mr Oakley, along with everyone else.

You can't get more authentic than that! thought Katy to herself.

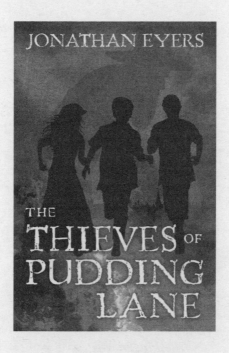

The Thieves of Pudding Lane
Jonathan Eyers

London, 1666.

Orphaned by the Great Plague, Sam is starving on the streets, until the desperate boy joins Uncle Jack's gang of thieves. If Sam is caught by the law, the punishment will be death - and if he crosses Uncle Jack, it could be even worse.

Still, it's a living for Sam and his partner in crime Catherine. Then a blaze at the Pudding Lane bakery runs out of control and, with London burning, the two thieves learn the true evil of Uncle Jack's schemes.

ISBN 978 1 4729 0318 1

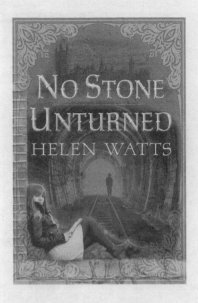

No Stone Unturned
Helen Watts

The past never goes away

Kelly, a Traveller, is isolated and unhappy at her new school.
Until the hot summer day when she meets Ben.

Ben offers to help Kelly with her local history project. It's just schoolwork
- except that the investigation quickly becomes compelling. Strange puzzles
are revealed. The quarry's dark secret is uncovered. Soon the mystery
of the past is spilling into the present - and into Kelly's own life.

Kelly must bring the long-buried truth to light. And she will
leave no stone unturned.

ISBN 978 1 4729 0540 6